The Flawless Life

by Serenity McLean

The Flawless Life

DOME TREE
Publishing

Published by Dome Tree Publishing

ISBN 978-0-9952721-1-8

© Serenity McLean, 2016

All Rights Reserved

First Edition August 2015

Second Edition August 2016

Requests for permission to use or reproduce material from this book should be directed to serenity@serenitymclean.com.

Author's Note

Don't worry about anything;
Instead, pray about everything.
Tell God what you need, and thank him for all he has done.
Then you will experience God's peace,
Which exceeds anything we can understand.
His peace will guard your hearts and minds
As you live in Christ Jesus.
Philippians 4:6–7

The Flawless Life is the story of confronting fear, desperation and panic. The main character Grace experiences an unexpected loss that sends her into panic. She pleads to God for help, but hears nothing. She begs and offers to live a better life. Still God seems silent.

I have personally experienced loss similar to Grace and at times have felt God was silent. And I have struggled with seeing myself as God sees me. The change in my thinking partially inspired this story. But I was also inspired by Bart Millard's story and how he expressed this same revelation in his music from MercyMe's album *Welcome to the New*. If you haven't heard his story, I have included links on my website to several of the videos and encourage you to watch them.

I hope this story inspires you to laugh on God's surfboard, and see the chaos in life as turtles.

Enjoy and blessings,

The Flawless Life

Acknowledgments

Thanks to the many who encouraged me along the way with the first book *Memory of Memories*. I continue to appreciate my mom who encourages and is my biggest fan – love you, Mom.

Thanks to my good friend Sarah McEvoy who generously offered her feedback and encouragement.

Thanks to my Hawaiian pastor JD Farag, for being my online pastor and contributing a message to my readers.

My great thanks to my editor Janet Dimond who both passed along improvement ideas and painstakingly pointed out all my errors.

In humble gratitude I thank The Word Guild for the honour of choosing this book as 2016 Finalist in the contemporary category.

Biggest thanks to my Lord who leads and directs in all things.

The Flawless Life

Contents

The Flawless Life

1 | The Day Desperation Came

September 22

Grace arrived early at work, as was her habit. Her boss scheduled an early meeting to talk about plans for the upcoming year, so she wanted to gather her thoughts and some papers in preparation.

As she neared her boss' office, she saw him talking to someone, so she stepped back to wait. He spotted her and called her in. As Grace entered, she felt the near-physical impact. This meeting was about her.

She knew the economy had affected the company, but every month management insisted they were finished with laying people off. Yet every month they packaged more people out. One by one the staff reduced, and here, this morning, was her time.

Experienced, they operated quickly. They ripped the bandage off in a matter of seconds, leaving her reeling. They walked her back to her office to gather her purse. The rest would be boxed up and sent to her. They collected her security cards and escorted her out the door. Done. Within ten minutes they completed their deed.

At the elevators she stood. Alone. Jobless.

Her heart pounded so hard, she felt it in her head. Her gut filled with anxiety. She felt sick. Her brain raced. *How will I provide for myself and Mom?* The room swam. *What in the world will I tell Mom? How can I tell her I lost my job? They said it was without cause, they didn't think they needed my skill set anymore. But what about the others who got shuffled to new roles? Am I not good enough? What had I done wrong? Why me?*

Then the wave of self-recrimination ploughed over. She felt completely worthless. *They don't want or need me anymore.*

One of her friends in the company arrived, and with one look at her took her across the street for a tea. She tried really hard not to let the tears take over, but they welled up as the emotions and turmoil overwhelmed what little control she had left.

She finally got a hold of herself enough to get to her car. With a deep breath she prayed, "God, I really need you. You know –" and with tears pouring out, she gulped, "I'm scared." She said nothing more. She turned on the radio and focused on the traffic. She could fall apart after she got home.

With determined focus she managed an uneventful trip home, navigating out of rote practice. As she pulled into the driveway, she gathered herself and gave a quick prayer. "Lord, give me your strength. I don't know what to say and I don't want to worry Mom."

Breathing out the tension, she turned off the car, walked to the door, let herself in, steadied her emotions, took a breath, and in her most cheerful voice announced her arrival home. Curious, her mom came out to meet her. The moment had come. She needed to be strong.

"Well, they have packaged me out. Over the last six months they reduced staff, and I guess I was next on the list."

Grace's mom, ever the practical one, and well seasoned by life, simply said, "God is in control. Does this mean you will be at home for awhile? You know I love it when you are home."

With a grateful smile she said, "Yes, this means I am home until I can find another job." Her mom gave her a big hug and asked if she would like a tea.

Well into her 80s, her mom struggled with memory loss and decreased cognitive function. Grace did not want to add to her stress, but clearly her mom trusted God without hesitation.

Her mom experienced this kind of trial of faith before. She told Grace about the time when they were a young family, her dad was unemployed for months on end and her mom became desperate. She said she became so desperate, she finally cried out in frustration to God, "Don't you know what we are going through here?"

Grace could sure relate to that.

Her mom said from her perspective she saw no way out, but God delivered a job in time. Not in loads of time, but in time. She learned faith and trust despite how things looked from a human vantage point. And she knew from a lifetime of experience walking with God, He always delivered.

Knowing this with your head, and really resting in faith and trusting God are two vastly different things, she thought. Yes, she believed in the Bible where He promised to look after His own. *If He cared for the sparrow, surely He will care for me.*

Well, she understood the promise, in concept. But "in concept" is definitely not the same as "in practice." She found it impossible to really believe it would be okay, when the weight and responsibility of looking after herself, her mom, the two dogs, and the mortgage overwhelmed her thoughts. Loomed. Dominated.

Over time, Grace read many verses of promise, trying to fill her head and heart with the truth, and get her focus on things above, but the responsibility, the weight of her reality would quickly pull her focus down to her earthly burdens. And this destruction of her determination would occur within a matter of minutes of trying to set her mind in the camp of belief and trust.

But on this first day, she couldn't allow her head to get mired in the black hole of desperation and despondency. Reading the Bible failed to conquer her fears. The loss of her job traumatized her deeply, leaving a fresh, open and very deep wound. Even if she managed to regain the slightest control over her thoughts, within moments her mind gushed fear.

For today, she didn't want to deal with fear, or the work of controlling her thoughts. She desperately needed a diversion. She watched the news for a few minutes, but needed something far more engaging, something pure entertainment, something she could lose herself in. She flipped through the guide, but there was nothing. She looked through the PVR.

No, what she needed was a good movie, maybe a comedy, something with a happy ending. So she moved onto Netflix and watched several movies that first day. She took a couple of Gravol to settle her stomach, which helped with a good night's sleep.

2 | The Silent God

September 23

She made it through that first day. The next morning she opened her email to find several people reached out to her to make sure she was okay. She closed her laptop, went to the kitchen to get a hot drink and consider how to answer these emails. Was she okay?

She took her tea back to her room and another wave of sobs washed over her. No, she was *not* okay. In fact, she felt worse today. Yesterday she lived in fear. Today filled with terror.

She opened her Bible and searched for verses with promises to keep and protect. She spent some time in the Psalms. She could really understand David in some of them. Yes, reading of David's struggle helped her mind. But she remained at a loss as to how to control her emotions. She could get her mind focused on God's promises, but then her unmanageable fear would wash over her mind like a tsunami, leaving her in a destroyed mess.

She responded to all those emails by simply saying, "I'm okay. Give me a few days to get myself together. Thank you so much for caring about me. Can we talk next week?" That would buy her a bit of time to gain some control.

She determined to take it one day at a time. The company gave her documents to review and sign to get the package they offered her. So she sat down to focus on the details. By the time she took off taxes, they offered the equivalent of six weeks. For under two years, this was more than they were legally required to give her. She signed and returned the paperwork.

She looked around the room. Now she had nothing else to focus on. And immediately came another tsunami. She quietly shut her bedroom door, buried her head in her pillow and let it all out. She sobbed for at least an hour. Her eyes swelled red. Her nose stuffed. And she had a pounding headache. The emotion steamrolled over her, but she let it. Now the landscape of her heart lay stripped bare, and the beach of her mind left barren except for the inevitable scraps of damage strewn everywhere.

That wave emptied her soul of emotion. All washed out to sea. She felt like a hollow shell. Depleted. Desolate. Drained.

Without the weighty burden of emotion, she should feel lighter, maybe even normal. But no. In letting the overpowering emotions crash over her and recede, she stripped herself of all emotion. She emptied her emotional bank. She now felt nothing. Numb.

No, she did feel something. Lifeless.

She pulled herself out of bed, and like a zombie walked to the bathroom to take a shower and clean herself up.

She welled up again and cried out her pain, but with it all the emotion washed out and left her heart cauterized. It was stripped bare and sealed up so the turmoil would not return. If closing her heart came as a package deal, well, so be it.

She went to the kitchen to figure out what they would have for dinner. They had an unwritten rule. Her mom cooked dinner when she went to work and she made dinner when home.

Shortly her mom joined her and quietly helped, knowing not to press.

She simply offered her companionship. In half an hour she put their dinner in the oven. Her mom made tea for both of them and they sat down together in the living room, looking out the window at the sunny day.

Eventually, her mom said, "What are you going to do with your trip to Hawaii?" Grace turned to look at her blankly. She forgot about her trip. She planned and saved for this trip for a year. With her flights and accommodations booked she knew it could be cancelled, but she couldn't get her money back.

Grace said, "I don't know. I forgot about it. Maybe I can sell it to someone."

She checked with the airlines and found she could transfer the tickets to someone else with additional charges. Four weeks remained for her to find someone to take her place. She sent a blanket email to all her contacts to see if anyone was interested in a single return ticket. Most replied they could not go. She waited a week, but no one said yes.

Her mom suggested Grace should go anyway. She already spent the money and the change of scenery would do her good. Certainly the Scot in her wanted value from the money already spent. And after all, it would be a great distraction.

So for the next three weeks, she split her time between looking for work and getting ready for her trip. She made sure her mom was set for the duration of the trip and would call her every day to make sure she was okay. One of her friends volunteered their time in case she needed someone to drop by and help her mom.

She still felt drained of all feeling. She pulled together a list of verses and chapters she knew were supportive for someone in her situation, and read them every day. And yes, she could hear her voice, her cry in those verses. But in a matter of verses, all seemed good again. When she finished reading these ancient words and looked at her world, it all seemed so disconnected. Her world was filled with desperation, almost hopelessness. And God seemed to be nowhere in sight. She felt she was totally alone, abandoned in the echoes of God's silence.

Years ago, in a spurt of faith, she prayed God would only open the doors she was meant to walk through, and keep closed all the others. For the first years after her prayer, her life painlessly progressed. New opportunities came along and she easily moved from one great job to the next, with barely an interview required.

But this time her situation differed vastly. She sent out resumes, contacted her network, and yet nothing came back as even a remote possibility. She saw no doors of opportunity, certainly no open doors. Just nothing.

No matter her prayers, her pleading, her Bible reading, her throwing God's promises at Him and demanding an answer, there was silence. She made conditional offers to do more at church, if He would get her a job. She promised to read her Bible every day. She promised to work harder at being a good Christian.

Still silence.

Numbly, she functioned at the basic level, concerned for food and shelter, and desperately concerned about employment. Love and belonging didn't matter, her self-respect long gone. She lived a long way from believing in who she really was and what she had to offer the world.

The emotional barrenness left a dark and lonely life inside, but Grace didn't care. The emptiness was okay. She couldn't cope with the onslaught of terror and fear. No, her heart would have to remain sealed, the walls remaining intact.

She held no anger against God. Instead, she felt cast adrift on a sea of no self-worth and no self-respect, an endless expanse called the Ocean of Failures.

Daily, she struggled to shut out negative thoughts, but she was spiralling out of control, getting sucked into a big black hole. Her internal life became a dark, joyless world. She had shut down. She called out to God daily, but felt nothing but emptiness. She ran out of new ideas. No doors opened. She felt lost and alone.

Not ready to completely give up her belief in God, she simply lost her faith in His interest in her and His willingness to come through for her.

This was not God's failure. Her conclusion – she failed at living a good enough Christian life and so didn't warrant God's hand of attention. She needed to find the key, the secret, to finally discover what would please Him and move Him to action. More prayer? More Bible reading?

Whatever it was, she would need to figure out what God wanted of her. And she needed to figure it out quickly. She didn't have much time. Living alone in this world and being responsible for her mom, she needed divine intervention, and soon. She couldn't make it on her own. This distant, removed, silent God was the only hope she had.

Bonus Content

Have you had a loss in your life? Did God seem silent? Share your thoughts! Go to serenitymclean.com/flawlessbonus/ and join the Silent God discussion.

The Flawless Life

3 | A Trip to Paradise

October 17

Grace woke early the morning of the flight. Her cab would be arriving shortly. Thankfully the air remained warm from the day before, as she dressed lightly for the Hawaiian weather. She gathered her passport, a good book to read and new music loaded on her phone.

She sat to wait for the cab. Alone with her thoughts, she began to think. *This is crazy. I have no job.* She saw nothing on the employment horizon, not even a remote possibility. *And here I am going to Hawaii, like all is well in my world.*

It is not well — it is not well with my soul either.

The cab pulled into her driveway and the cabby helped her with her suitcases. The ride to the airport took half an hour and she spent it with her head on the window, looking at the passing houses. Thankfully the cabby didn't feel the need to chat.

Her flight from Victoria to Vancouver took another half hour, then another couple of hours layover before catching the flight to Hawaii.

Once in Vancouver, she passed through international security faster than she expected and found a quiet place near the gate to get comfortable and start her book. Occasionally she looked over the gathering crowd, checking out the people she would be spending the next several hours with. As soon as she thought, *Good, no babies,* along came a young couple with piles of gear and a baby in a stroller, heading to the gate. *Great. Six hours with a screaming baby. Fantastic.*

Sighing, she returned to her book. The story seemed to be good, but the distractions outside the windows commanded her attention. The business of air travel seemed a good diversion. Aircraft moved about in the distance. Planes were towed in and out of the neighbouring gates. Luggage was loaded onto her plane, while more luggage was taken out of the next one.

The sky began to lighten with the sun ready to break over the horizon. Grace loved a good sunrise and sunset, so was happy to watch the slow change of colours. The sky worked its way through the colour palette from dark blue, purple, red, orange, yellow and finally a light blue of a fresh, clear autumn morning.

They already called for advanced boarding and for people in the back rows. Grace packed her jacket in her carry-on, and got her ticket and passport organized. She was seated two seats ahead of the wings, so she would probably be the last group to board. Hopefully the baby would be somewhere near the back. She intended to get her ear buds in and blast the music at the first hint of crying.

She booked a window seat and hoped staring out the window would signal to the world she was little interested in conversation. Once onboard, she settled quickly and got her book open to really make it clear – no intention of chatting. Eventually no new people boarded the plane and the two seats next to her remained empty. Maybe she had lucked out.

Rather than watch people get settled, Grace chose to look out the window. Most people were seated and still no one sat in the seats next to her. Then another passenger boarded. She glanced to the front to see a woman who paused to talk to the flight attendant. They both turned and looked right at her. She knew this would be her seatmate for the flight.

She looked nice enough. She appeared a little older than Grace and wore a gentle but competent look on her face. As this woman made her way down the aisle, she looked at Grace, meeting her eyes. She smiled and greeted her warmly.

Okay, if I have to have a seatmate, this seems like a good one.

After finding a spot for her carry-on, she turned to settle in. They both looked forward at the noise of the plane door closing. She smiled at Grace and said, "Looks like we have a spare seat." Stretching out her hand, she said, "Hi, my name is Connie."

Grace shook her hand and said, "Hi, I'm Grace."

Connie sat down and started hunting for the two halves of the seatbelt, then stood to find them. Once seated, she turned to Grace and said, "So, are you visiting Hawaii on vacation? Or do you live there?"

Kind of surprised, Grace thought, *Who would ever leave Hawaii to be visiting here?* She said, "I am going for a two-week vacation. And you?"

With a sigh Connie said, "I was born and raised in Hawaii. I left when I got married, but my dad still lives there. He fell last week and broke his leg, so he needs a bit of help with his business. I am going for a few weeks to help him out. Where on the island will you be staying?"

"I've rented a little cottage in Kailua about three streets off the beach. Do you know the area?"

"Yes, Kailua is where my dad lives. Are you staying close to Kalama? Actually, the entire area has such great beaches and is not as busy as Waiki-ki. Winds prevail on the windward coast producing more waves, but I don't mind the waves and prefer it less busy."

And so they chatted for quite awhile. They discovered they had much in common. Both now lived in Victoria, both were living single and neither had any children.

When the attendant came by with tea and coffee, Grace had a moment to herself and was surprised she had actually enjoyed the conversation. She'd been so determined to remain alone in her internal world, but without being aware, she let herself relate to someone in the real world. It felt good.

They chatted off and on throughout the flight, through deboarding and the walk to pick up their luggage. She found she really liked Connie. She could see them becoming friends and was ready to suggest they look each other up when they both got back from Hawaii. But Connie beat her to it.

"Grace, I don't mean to intrude on your vacation, but if you are available for dinner, maybe we could go to one of the local haunts?"

Distracted by collecting her suitcase, and without thinking through her answer, she said, "I have no plans at all. Dinner would be great."

Still watching for her luggage, Connie said, "Okay, well, here is my dad's phone number and address." She pulled out one of her business cards and wrote on the back. "How about tomorrow night? How can I reach you?"

"I don't know if there is a phone at the rental, but let me give you my email." She scribbled her contact information on a scrap receipt. "You can iMessage me at this number if you have an iPhone. And tomorrow would be great. Thanks, Connie. See you tomorrow."

"Say, how are you getting to Kailua? Did you rent a car?"

She had cancelled her rental to save some money. "No, I planned on waiting for the bus."

Grabbing her two cases off the carousel, Connie said, "Want a lift? My uncle is picking me up and we would be happy to drop you off."

"You sure?" Connie vigorously nodded and Grace said, "If you are sure, a lift would be great." *This will save some money.*

"Positive. Come on, I'm pretty sure he will be waiting. He's a diehard surfer and if the waves are up, he'll be happy to get back as soon as possible."

Hmm. This should be interesting, an old surfer dude. Smiling, she wondered if they would be travelling in an old VW wagon painted hippie. Then it occurred to her. Today was the first day she had smiled or had a random amusing thought in a long time. It indeed felt good.

As they turned to head to the pickup area, a momentary worry flashed through her mind. *What am I doing? I don't know this woman and never met the man who will be driving. I'm in a different country. And I'm alone. If they intend evil, it will be two against one. This could turn out to be a dangerous decision.* She slowed a little to sneak a good look at Connie without her knowing, and gave a quick prayer. *God, please, if this is dangerous, let me know right now. Please don't be silent on this one.*

Quickly studying Connie for any signal to confirm or alleviate her concern, she really gave her a thorough looking over. And then she noticed the tags on her suitcase. Connie had metal tags of the Christian fish symbol on each case. Once she noticed those, she felt a confirmation in her heart. No harm would come to her.

Stepping outside, the warm, moist air blasted her face and arms. *Oh, this feels great.* She breathed deeply, filling her lungs with the humid Hawaiian air. She paused to take a look around. Beautiful green palm trees as far as the eye can see. She could feel a crack in the cold blackness of her soul. She silently thanked her mom. *Yes, this will be good for me.*

Connie said, "Ah, Jeff!" and headed straight for a fully restored classic surf wagon, a woody. She almost laughed out loud. Awesome! Connie's uncle got out to greet her warmly. Clearly this family loved each other, regardless of time and distance.

Didn't Connie call him her uncle? He looked a bit younger than Connie and was wearing classic surfer dude T-shirt, shorts and flip-flops. After joshing Connie a bit, he stepped back and Connie did introductions. "Grace, let me introduce you to my rogue Uncle Jeff. Watch out. He's pure trouble looking for a place to happen."

In response to Connie's teasing, Jeff shoved her aside, stepped up to Grace and said, "I'm not trouble, I'm fun looking for a place to happen. Pleased to meet you, Grace," with Connie mocking him and mouthing his exact words in sync from behind him.

"Ignore her," he said, pointing to Connie behind him without looking back. She laughed at their antics. "Are you a friend of Connie's? Will you be staying with Connie and Joe?"

"No, we met on the plane. I have rented a small place in Kailua and Connie generously offered your taxi services."

"Ah, well then, my ladies, hop in and I will get your luggage." Opening the front door he said, "Here Grace, sit up front with me. I know Connie and she'll probably sleep. Come sit with me and keep me company."

Looking back, Connie nodded in agreement and waved her into the front seat.

Once they cleared the airport and were travelling along the highway, Jeff asked if they would mind a stop at Starbucks. Connie eagerly agreed and they turned off the highway.

While waiting in line Jeff asked if Grace had visited Hawaii before. She shook her head and he proceeded to talk about the island and the great sites to see. The conversation weaved around swimming with turtles and dolphins, scenic hiking trails and of course, surfing.

Back in the woody, he chatted about growing up in Kailua. Grace turned around to ask Connie if she grew up surfing, but she was lying down in the back, eyes closed, her breathing slow and steady. Grace turned back grinning and said, "Out like a light."

Jeff viewed life in an amusing way and told entertaining stories of his and Connie's youth. She found out Connie's father owned a popular burger joint and Jeff owned a couple of surf shops.

Apparently, Connie's grandmother adopted a baby Hawaiian girl when Connie's mom had married. When her grandmother passed away five years after the adoption, Connie's mom raised Kim alongside Connie as a sister. Jeff married Connie's young Aunt Kim, but Kim had passed away almost two years ago with breast cancer.

Jeff and Kim had raised two boys to early adulthood when Kim passed. One finished university and lived on the mainland in San Francisco, working in advertising and marketing. The other boy was currently finishing a co-op term at the Hawaii Institute of Marine Biology, living at home and would be returning to California in a month.

He seemed pretty proud of his boys, and she wondered how often he would see them once they settled with wives on the mainland.

Jeff laughed easily and it struck her how he expressed genuine and authentic happiness. She marvelled at how he moved past his loss and wondered how long it takes to emotionally recover from the black hole. He seemed so easygoing, contented and open to the world. Not the shut down person she was becoming. Sure, nearly two years passed, but she couldn't detect any scars. And he lost far more than she could imagine.

She looked out the window at the amazing scenery as they headed into the mountains. With a break in the conversation, she had a moment with her own thoughts. She really liked Connie and Jeff. They seemed good people. Perhaps divine intervention put them together on the plane. She decided to encourage a friendship with Connie. She too had a happy face and an easygoing manner. She felt comfortable and relaxed with her.

And then there was Jeff. On the surface he looked like a shallow surfer dude, but she sensed those waters ran deep. He seemed very generous with his time, and well, with himself.

He broke into her thoughts and asked what she did for a living. She instantly tensed. She looked straight ahead and said, "I worked as a project manager, but with the recession my company packaged me out. Right now I'm between jobs and looking. Companies offer little opportunity because of the economy."

There. She said it without any emotion slipping out. No welling tears. No catch in her voice. She took a deep breath and relaxed. She would be okay.

"That's tough," he said. "Loss can be very hard to rise above."

Oh no, not sympathy. If there's too much sympathy, I'll fall apart. She wanted to avoid the humiliation of sobbing into a puddle in front of these people she hoped would become her friends. No one wanted a crying woman on their hands. They would think she was unstable.

They were both quiet for awhile, then Jeff said, "Grace, do you believe in Yehovah God?"

Well, she thought pivoting to God an unusual turn in the conversation. Religion, generally considered a taboo subject, would be an easier topic than her work. Well, perhaps slightly better. Probably she could talk about God without gushing tears.

"Yes. I grew up going to church every week. I abandoned it in university and lived my own way for a few years, but came back to living as a Christian. I don't really go to church now, but I still believe."

He turned to look at her while she answered, glancing occasionally at the highway. He focused the majority of his attention on her, listening intently to her answer. She wondered what he studied her for. It felt like he saw past her walls of protection and deep inside her soul.

Normally, she kept her private self quite private and didn't let anyone in. But here, a virtual stranger easily navigated past all her walls and barriers and hit no resistance. She felt quite relaxed with both Connie and Jeff and didn't feel he was too invasive. Maybe because she knew him only as a stranger, she opened herself to talking about her closely guarded inner self.

With an easy smile he said, "I gather, 'I don't really go to church' means you don't go at all?"

Laughing, she said, "Yes, but I do watch a weekly service on YouTube. Actually, it is broadcast from Kaneohe and I thought I might try to get to the real service while here."

"You must be speaking of JD, my Hawaiian shirt pastor! I often go there myself. I can take you, if you like."

"Really? That would be great." She wouldn't have to sit alone. Eating alone and going to church alone. Two things she disliked. She really didn't mind being alone, and in fact sought out quite a bit of alone time. But she didn't like sitting with a bunch of people who are together in a social setting when she was alone.

"So you are one of the 20,000 who watch his prophesy updates. What do you think?"

"Oh, I love his updates. I really look forward to them each week. I think time is ticking steadily onward, but the events on the timeline have really sped up. The prophetic events fill the news now. The huge story of several days ago seems like a long time ago because so many new huge stories have occurred since. It's like JD says, the birth pangs are now coming hard and fast. And that can only mean one thing –"

"We're out of here soon," he said, finishing her sentence. "I think so too."

The remainder of the trip was filled with conversation about current events in the world, how they align with the Bible, and what they thought about the real critical markers to watch.

The time passed quickly and easily. She loved talking with him because he was so much like her in many ways.

He asked the address of her rental, and after a couple of questions determined they should stop at a grocery store to get some food. Connie took the opportunity to get some groceries for her and her dad. She was relieved they weren't stopping just for her.

Jeff pulled up to the small rental and helped her with her suitcases and Connie helped with the groceries.

Grace turned to thank them both, and Connie gave her a warm hug and said, "Don't forget about dinner tomorrow night. How about I pick you up around 7 p.m.?"

"Sounds good, only I didn't think I would be going out with anyone and didn't bring anything more than shorts and jeans."

With a big smile Connie said, "No worries. I only do the fancy kind of dining once a year. We're good. See you tomorrow!"

She turned to thank Jeff and he gave her a hug as well. So she gave him a warm hug back. He really did feel like a good friend, and it broke through to the black hole and started to melt the icy numbness in her heart. She found this a safe place to regain herself. Here in Hawaii she could forget her dilemma for awhile, and just be herself. Connie and Jeff were safe people.

She put the groceries away and her suitcases in the bedroom, then decided to walk down to the beach. She packed her wallet and camera, checked the map and was out the door.

This was the first time she decided to rent a small house instead of staying in a hotel or motel, and felt the difference immediately. She already felt a part of the place and quickly slid into feeling like a resident. With the hotel thing she always felt like a tourist, a person apart from the place.

She expected to really feel like an outsider, here alone in a house, separated from other vacationers like herself. But she really felt welcomed, comfortable and a part of the place. Certainly not lonely.

She had looked forward to the alone time, the separated isolation because of the black hole in her heart. She considered her change from isolation to friendship with Connie and Jeff on her way to the beach, and thought she saw God's hand all over it. *Maybe He does watch over my life, even if from a distance.*

Grace slowly made her way along the side streets to the beach and found everything lush with greenery, including the beach entry. She got out her digital SLR camera to take a few photos. With little prior experience with this new camera, it took her awhile to get all the settings, but the results pleased her.

At a little past 5 p.m., she saw a few people out surfing and a smattering of people on the beach. She walked down to the water's edge and took off her flip-flops, packing them in her small backpack.

Oh, the water was fabulous, warm as it tickled across her toes and up her feet. Looking at the changing line between water and sand, she noted the waves failed to reach the full distance of the wet sand. *The tide must be going out.*

She spotted a small beach concession stand ahead and bought some iced tea and nacho chips. She walked a distance from the stand to ensure she would remain alone and settled in the warmth of the beach to take in the sand, surf and sky, and to contemplate her life.

After a quick prayer over her meal, Grace paused. *God, are you really here? Right here beside me? Thank you for Connie and Jeff. I hope Connie and I can continue our friendship when we both get back home. Thank you for inserting some warmth into my broken heart. I am still very scared, Lord. Please don't warm my heart for me to face terror again.* After a long, quiet pause she prayed, *What do I need to do to move You to action? I won't leave you, but I am really struggling.*

She had nothing more to say. With her eyes filled with the evidence of her pain, she looked out at the water. Blurry through her tears, she sighed deeply, blinked a couple of times and wiped her tears away. Looking up and down the beach, the lack of people comforted her.

She let out a breath to rid herself of the emotions and took a drink of her iced tea. She slowly ate through her chips. She watched how the waves reduced to bubbling foam as they stretched their way up the sand. She noticed the patterns as the water receded back to the ocean at different speeds, leaving lines of foam. She counted the waves between big waves to see if there was any truth to the one in seven rumour. She concluded it was a myth.

After a long time of studying the water, she realized the beauty mesmerized her and broke her gaze to look around. Few people remained on the beach. She gathered up her things and again walked along the water's edge. She took several pictures of the patterns of foam, wet sand, and even her footprints in it. She liked those ones – evidence of her life, her presence.

With the sun quite low in the sky behind the land, she decided to head back, diverting through Kailua Beach Park. She took a few photos of the sun through the palms. She turned back to the ocean and took a number of photos through the palms with the beautiful sky beginning its slow progress to night.

Once back at the house, she copied her images to her tablet. Looking them over on the larger screen, she found most turned out beautifully.

Exhausted from the day's travels, she decided to go to bed early. *If I wake up early, I can go back down to the beach to take some sunrise shots. The Kailua coast faces east. It might be a pretty morning.*

She gave her mom a quick call and promised to call every few days

The Flawless Life

then headed for bed.

4 | The Door Cracks Open

October 18

Grace awoke before sunrise still on mainland time. The spectacular sunrise and warm, humid air kept her on the beach taking many photos until mid-morning. She returned to the house for a late breakfast and packed for an afternoon on the beach.

Swimming and relaxing in the warm sand warmed her soul. She slept a couple of hours in the sun, setting her up to stay awake through dinner tonight with Connie.

She always tanned quickly. An English friend, who would go from white to red and back to white, once said in frustration, "You get a tan just looking at a travel brochure."

And in one afternoon her skin took on the hue of a native. She smiled to herself. Not only was she feeling like a resident, now she looked like she belonged.

A few minutes remained before she expected Connie and she thought about her day. *I really feel okay. Almost like a living being.*

She spent the day alone with nature. Retreating there always grounded her. She worked through the tough moments of her life when she could leave people behind and really connect with creation. And today was a balm to her soul.

She snapped out of her introspective thoughts when she heard the car pull up, grabbed her backpack and keys, and headed out. After locking up she turned to discover Jeff holding the car door for her. A little puzzled, she thought it would be only her and Connie.

Grinning at him she said, "Ah, Connie sent trouble to come get me."

Holding a finger up, with a fake stern look on his face, he corrected her. "No, no. Not trouble. I thought I told you I'm fun looking for a place to happen. Hop in. Connie got back from Joe's office late and asked if I'd come pick you up in exchange for dinner with you two. She went back to check on Joe and said she'll meet us at the restaurant. Hope you don't mind me joining you."

Smiling warmly she said, "Not at all, Jeff. The more the merrier and you just promised us some fun," and hopped in the front seat. She smiled. He felt like a brother.

Once at the wheel he asked what kind of food she liked. She answered, "Almost everything," and asked if there was a place the locals really liked.

He said, "Do you like sushi or Korean?"

"I love both. Either way is fine with me. You pick."

"Sushi it is. We can go to Connie's favourite restaurant," and off they went. The restaurant seemed pretty full and there was a lineup, but Jeff went to the front to speak with the hostess. Clearly they knew each other and after a brief exchange, he waved at her to follow him. They headed to a private booth in a quiet section. They removed their shoes and sat down at a zashiki-style low table on a sunken floor. He excused himself while he texted Connie where to meet them.

Shortly, a plate of California rolls arrived and they chatted like two old friends. They laughed freely and she found herself quick on her feet, easily keeping up with him. She brought him to laughter as much as he did for her. She asked about his surf shop business and how he got into it, his boys, and if he travelled much from paradise. Almost an hour passed without either of them noticing.

When he realized this, he was a little concerned about Connie and called her, but got no answer. He called the house and got Joe on the phone. Grace could hear Joe's voice and realized it was nothing too serious, and relaxed. After a quick conversation he said, "Joe said Connie got home and took a quick shower. She sat for a couple of minutes to talk over some business items with him, then leaned back for a moment and promptly fell asleep. I'm sorry, Grace. I don't think Connie will be joining us tonight. She is going to be mortified when she wakes up and realizes she missed her date with us. Looks like it is only you and me."

They ordered their meal and thoroughly enjoyed an evening of fun, laughter and good conversation, all the things of good friendship. When he dropped her off, he walked around to open the car door and walked her to the house. She thanked him for a wonderful evening, and he hugged her again and said, "You are welcome, my dear. I am sure Connie is going to want to make it up to you. Are you busy tomorrow evening? Maybe we could all go for Korean?"

She pretended to weigh the options and said, "Well, I am pretty booked up with all my masses of friends, but I guess I can spare tomorrow evening." She hardly got it out when they both laughed.

"Okay, I will pick you up around 7 p.m. tomorrow. Have a good night and a good day tomorrow."

"'Night Jeff, and thanks."

After checking her email for jobs, she lay in bed thinking about the day and turned to pray. *God, thank you for placing good people in my path. My soul benefited from this day. But this is only for two weeks, then this dream is over and I go back to face my world, my dark, black, bleak world. What do I need to do to move you to actually do something?*

Silence.

Okay, I appreciate the break. I appreciate the friendship, but you know what? I would rather a job than another friend. Here I sit in paradise having a good time, when in reality I hold the bitter end of my rope. No more rope. I feel it a little cruel to give me a piece of paradise with good people, then rip it all away to face financial desperation and no opportunity. It's just not fair.

And she fell asleep with hot tears in her eyes.

October 19

Grace got up late the next morning. She sat on the lanai out back and read her Bible for quite awhile. She made herself a bite to eat, then spent the afternoon at the beach.

She spent the day specifically avoiding any thought about how great her days were in this paradise, or any thought about how grim a life she faced on returning home. She focused on the moment, the immediate and superficial.

In fact, she enjoyed another great day at the beach. She figured her worry was making no difference to her future, so best she stay in the moment. Contented at the beach, contented in the ocean, contented with her new friends, contented to be alone. Whatever.

Sure enough, right at 7 p.m. Jeff pulled up. He brought Connie with him this time. He got out to open the door for her and said, "I went to Joe's restaurant to collect Connie, took her home to get ready, and didn't let her sit down. No chance to fall asleep this time."

Connie turned around to look at Grace in the back seat. "Oh Grace, I am totally embarrassed. I never miss my appointments. I am never late. I feel really bad because I've never made a date with anyone, then slept through it. Please accept my apologies."

"No worries. Jeff told me a bit about all you're doing for your dad. I don't blame you at all. You're generous to share your time."

Jeff said, "Well, let's go out and have a good evening together." Glancing at Grace in the rearview mirror, he said, "We'll leave behind all our worries and have some fun. Agreed?"

She had a momentary sense he knew exactly what she was thinking and feeling, but put this thought aside.

Both Grace and Connie agreed and they spent the evening laughing and sharing stories of work, home and life. They enjoyed a great meal and she found herself actually happy, living in the moment.

Connie said, "Grace, I plan on spending tomorrow at home. I want some time with Dad to prepare some of his favourite meals for his freezer. Would you like to come over and meet my dad, and let me make you dinner to make up for missing our dinner date last night?"

She hesitated. *These folks generously spent so much time with me already. Surely their calendars were filled with other people they would rather be with?*

Unseen by Grace, Jeff looked at Connie and slightly nodded toward Grace, a silent encouragement to Connie to press Grace a little harder. Connie nodded back, turned to Grace and said, "Grace, I really want to make it up to you and it would be good to have your company. Pick you up at 6 p.m.?"

She realized Connie felt pretty badly and really wanted to apologize for missing dinner, so she agreed.

Jeff walked her to the door and wished her a good night, squeezing her shoulder before turning back to the car. "See you tomorrow," he said before getting into the driver's seat. She waved good-bye to her two new friends.

She popped open her tablet to refresh her mind about the buses she would take the next day to get to Sea Life Park and when she'd need to leave to get back in time. She knew it was touristy, but she might never be here again and she did love animals.

October 20

Grace headed off quite early the next morning, successfully finding her way to the bus stop. She enjoyed her day, getting a number of shots of people, particularly kids, animals, a few of trees and gardens, and lots of aquatic animals. She got back with enough time for a quick shower. She was finishing up when Jeff pulled up. She didn't have time to empty her backpack from her day trip, but grabbed it and ran out the door.

Once in the car, Grace and Jeff talked about each of their day's events for the quick five-minute trip.

She had not thought about the implications of owning a popular burger joint, but as Jeff navigated through the streets, it finally dawned on her.

These people lived a wealthy lifestyle. As they took several neighbourhood streets, the homes increased in size and grandeur. They finally turned onto Kailuana Loop and into the driveway of one of the waterfront mansions. She began to feel overwhelmed, and a wee bit out of her element.

Jeff, noticing her quiet, turned off the engine, looked at her and said, "You okay? You know, we have not morphed into aliens because we live in big homes. We are the two people you have eaten with and laughed with. Nothing has changed because of where we live."

"Yeah," she said, a bit distracted, staring at the huge house, gardens and three garages.

He got out and made his way around to get the door for her when Connie came out to greet them. Connie caught the look on her face. She knew that look, learning it early in childhood. "Aloha, Grace. I hope you like lasagna. It's Dad's favourite."

Oh no. This is going from bad to worse. "I do like lasagna, but I am gluten intolerant and cannot have anything with wheat in it. I am sorry, Connie. I should have said something before you went to all the work of preparing a meal."

With a bright look Connie said, "Perfect! Both Justin, Jeff's son, and I are celiac as well, so it is a totally gluten-free meal. I don't normally mention it because it tastes the same as regular lasagna. Come on in. I want to introduce you to Dad and Justin."

In a flush of guilt, she thought she should have brought something, a bottle of wine, or something. And that added to her growing feeling of being totally out of her element. But it seemed Connie read her mind. "I am so glad you didn't feel obliged to bring anything. This evening is all about me making it up to you for standing you up."

Connie told Jeff the lads were out on the lanai. "Please take Grace out there to meet Dad and Justin. Help yourself to the appetizers and drinks."

Grace turned to ask Connie if she could help with preparations, but she said everything was done and she would be right out. So Grace followed Jeff through the house. The rooms were spacious and well appointed. They came to open French doors looking out to lush greenery with the beach and ocean beyond.

"Grace, this is Joe. I consider him my father-in-law and Connie's dad. He has been my business mentor since I thought about opening a surf shop and is one of my best friends. Joe, this is Grace, our new friend from the mainland. Grace is here vacationing for a couple of weeks. Connie met Grace on the flight down."

After greeting Joe he said, "Grace, this is my youngest son Justin. I have another four weeks or so with him at home before he heads back for his last semester at university in California. We live along Kaneohe Bay, making it a quick trip to the Marine Research Center."

Justin offered to get her a drink, handed her a plate for the appetizers and made sure to offer her all the various appetizer dishes. She could see a lot of Jeff in him. Clearly Jeff and his wife raised children they could be proud of.

Lively conversation skipped along. Both Jeff and Justin kept Connie on her toes. After dinner Justin left to spend the rest of the evening with his friends. As Grace and Connie cleaned up the last dish, Jeff asked if they would like to take a walk down to the beach. Grace immediately accepted. She loved the sand and water. Connie declined, saying she wanted to spend some time relaxing on the lanai. Tea and coffee would be ready when they got back.

Normally, she would be a little suspicious of how things seemed to be working out for her and Jeff to be together, but she didn't get that kind of vibe from him. She believed he was into their friendship and nothing more, as was she.

They walked along quietly for quite awhile, content to listen to the ocean and be with each other. Finally, Jeff said, "Grace, tell me if I am getting too personal, but I sense you are really going through a rough patch right now."

She could feel the tears springing to her eyes, and bit her lips to hold back the tide of pain.

He waited a moment then continued. "I've been through a rough patch myself and wanted to spend some time sharing with you how hard it was to lose my wife. We were both Christians and went to church every week dutifully. When Kim died, my heart ripped out of me. The black loneliness overwhelmed me. I struggled to get up every morning. And I spent my days totally feeling barren. I didn't care what happened to my business. Both boys were at university, so no reason existed for me to join the land of the living. I buried the best part of me when I buried my sweet Kim."

They continued walking, but she could sense he had turned to look at her. "I can see the same hollowness in you, and wondered if you wanted to talk about it with someone who has returned from the blackness."

Tear overflowed her eyes. Her nose filled. She knew if she said anything, she'd lose all control. She sniffed and took a deep breath. He waited, quietly patient.

She looked up to the sky, sucked in a deep breath, slowly let it out and started. "My mom lives with me. It's just her and I. I've been packaged out of my job. And there are no opportunities. I applied to everything. I let my network know I am looking, but every door is solidly shut. I found no opportunity anywhere. I know we're supposed to trust God, but I don't see Him. I don't hear Him. I don't feel Him. I feel alone and don't know what more He wants of me. I feel like a maze rat, trying to figure out what button I have to push to get His attention and favour. It's not like we have much money. And I'm responsible for Mom and me, and all I see ahead is failure. I feel I am a big fat —" and she totally broke down. She felt foolish, but was beyond control and decided she was beyond caring.

He turned and pulled her in to hug her, and she sobbed in his arms. He pulled out several tissues from his pocket. *How had he known?* He waited until the sobbing faded, then put his arm around her shoulders and led her to a quiet place to sit in the still-warm sand, sheltered by palm trees.

He quietly said, "You know, I questioned whether Yehovah even cared that He took the best part of my life from me. He seemed pretty silent as I became increasingly morose. My world had fallen apart. I threw in His face all I had done for Him, and yet here He ripped my heart out. And all I got back was silence.

"I walked away from the Church and wanted to be left alone. I ignored calls from the church folks. I determined to stick with Yehovah, but really wanted nothing more to do with all the rules and all the church requirements, all the demands of the Christian life.

"I decided if I squeaked into heaven, well, I'd be okay with that. But I finished trying to be a great Christian. The world would need to find its own way to Christ. I no longer cared to be a fine Christian leader and strive to be the perfect husband, father, businessman and exemplary Christian.

"My disengagement lasted for many months. Thankfully, Joe stepped in and helped with my business. I spent my time surfing the waves. I couldn't buy into the whole Christian church thing anymore.

"Then one day I read Galatians and I was knocked off my feet. The truth hit me like a 30 ft. wave. I felt thrown underwater and couldn't tell up from down. All I had thought about my Christian life totally turned on its head.

"Yeah, I knew all the buzz words and critical verses, and yet I never saw the simple truth. I never understood it at all.

"Here's the truth, Grace. Yeshua Christ set us free. The work was completed at the cross. It really doesn't matter what I do or say. At my very worst, He still loved me exactly the same as He did on what I thought was my best day. The truth is, Grace, no matter what bruises, scars, the depth of hurt or pain, or even how angry I am, Yehovah still loves me, exactly the same. But even more than He loves me – He looks at me and sees me as flawless.

"All these thoughts I had of trying to measure up, to earn His approval, they are not from Yehovah. He tells us the opposite. The cross is all that is required. You simply need to believe in His completed work. That's it. That's all. You and I can walk in total freedom. We are truly carefree because of His grace making us spotless, sinless, and it was completed 2,000 years ago.

"I accepted Him into my life, but I picked up all these religious rules, things I thought I needed to do. I thought I needed to do these things to 'work out my salvation.' But the Bible specifically tells us to leave our burden at the cross and walk in freedom, not to become a slave to new burdens, or old burdens, for that matter. Specifically, it points to religious practice and tells us not to become slaves to the law.

"In terms of winning Yehovah's love, nothing I did influenced Him because nothing I did or could do would make Him love me any more. He already loved me with the full breadth and depth that can be found only in Yehovah. He already made me flawless. He required nothing more as He already committed to me and poured out His love on me daily.

"Grace, I still don't know why Kim was taken, but the fact is, I live in His grace. I live in freedom. No matter what anyone says or anything you think about yourself, you really are flawless, not a failure. God sees beautiful beyond imagination when He looks at you.

"A friend gave me some links to videos to watch, and a recommendation to buy a particular album, and to listen, really listen, to the message. I did. And the message took a hold of me. It welled up in my heart, my cold, lifeless heart, and filled me with a whole new perspective. That made me the man you see today. I still carry the shine of a new creature and I will carry that shine for eternity.

"Since our drive back from the airport, Yehovah has been speaking to me about you. I think this is a message you need to hear. Grace, no matter what you see around you, no matter what you see inside you, it's not what

Yehovah sees. He sees you as flawless and wants you to be dancing in His freedom. Trust and faith are so much easier when you drop all your worries and burdens at the completed work of the cross. And He has made provision with His grace so we can live in this freedom without care or worry.

"Grace, did I read it right? Is this something you needed to hear?"

She quietly nodded, totally broken before her God.

"Can I pray with you?"

She swallowed hard and squeaked out a yes.

He took her hand and said, "Our loving Father, Grace and I come before you with a whole mess of worry and burden. She feels she's been carrying this burden alone and is now overwhelmed. She feels lost and alone. She is in the same black place where you and I met last year. We come before you now asking you to pull the scales from her eyes and let her see the truth in the burden-free grace you offer. Father, let her see how you made her flawless and unstained in your eyes, and nothing she does can make you love her any more. Show her how much you cherish her and value her decision to believe in you. Show her how you never intended for her to carry any of these burdens beyond the cross. Show her how to drop it all and dance in your gracious freedom. In Yeshua's name we thank you. Amen.

"Grace, as one of my favourite songs by MercyMe says, we are one of the redeemed. And as a redeemed spirit, we are holy and righteous with a brand new heart. You are free. So, let me welcome you to the freedom. You will experience such a relief. Grace, I can't dance worth a bean, but my heart filled with an unbelievable joy. I am truly happy. At first, I needed to daily drop my pain at the cross, but in time I found myself living in His freedom. Yeah, I can take on the worry, but He told me He's got me, I am good. All I do is let it all go and live knowing He loves and cares for me regardless of how grim my day looks."

After giving her a moment to think, he said, "How are you doing? What are you thinking?"

With a big sniff, then a blow into her one remaining tissue, she took a breath and said, "I really want His freedom. I don't know how. Can you send me the links to the videos?"

"Sure." After a companionable silence he said, "Do you have plans for tomorrow? Can I take you surfing?"

Laughing out loud she said, "I have no plans and I love to spend time in the water, but I have never tried surfing. I may suck at it. You know I am no spring chicken anymore."

"Ah, it doesn't matter. Tell you what. I will dance on the beach in daylight if you will give surfing a try. And remember, I can't dance."

"I will hold you to your promise. Just so we are clear, the deal is I only need to try, but you must deliver. Seems fair."

He got up and offered his hand to help her up. "I will even sweeten the deal. I will dance on the beach, in daylight, in front of Connie and Joe, if you will give surfing a good try, that is, more than one try. Deal?"

Getting up she said, "Deal." They headed back along the beach, talking and laughing as best friends. As they neared the house, he asked if she was ready. She went to the water's edge and scooped cool water over her puffy eyelids and wiped them dry with her balled-up Kleenex. "Yup, ready – Wait – Jeff, thank you. I don't want to start crying again, but I want you to know I really appreciate you sharing your experience with me. It does feel good knowing someone journeyed ahead of me on the path. 'Kay, let's go."

They walked up the path to the house, laughing and teasing each other. Connie heard them coming and got the tea and coffee, and a platter of fresh island fruit.

Positive she still looked puffy from her crying despite the cool water, she gratefully felt relieved to not blubber in front of a bunch of people, having to explain the evidence of tears. At least on the beach it was dark and the horrible details of crying couldn't be closely observed.

They all chatted late into the evening, and finally Joe struggled to his feet to go to bed. Jeff helped him up, then asked Grace if she was ready to go.

She thanked both Joe and Connie for having her for dinner, and headed out to the car with Jeff.

As they neared her rental, she was digging through her backpack for her phone to take down Jeff's email. She was serious about following up on the videos he had recommended, and would send him an email so he could send her the links. Still rummaging in her backpack, they turned onto her street and Jeff stopped abruptly, causing her to look up. Emergency personnel blocked the entire street off. "Oh no," she said.

"Stay here, Grace. I'll go find out what is going on."

She could see him talking with a police officer and could tell they knew each other. He walked back to the car and got in. "Grace, I'm sorry, but the house next to where you're staying burned down, and there's smoke and extensive water damage to your place. It's uninhabitable and you can't stay there. Speaking with John," nodding toward the police officer, "he said he would get one of the firefighters to retrieve what they can from the house for you. It'll take a few minutes, but they should be back with some of your stuff they can salvage."

Looking at Grace, he pulled her close to him and wrapped his arm around her. "Grace, you know when you make steps in Yehovah's direction, you can count on opposition. This is Satan trying to bring you down. Yehovah is still in control and He can turn even the worst thing into something great. Don't lose hope. He's got you and you are good."

Grace leaned her head back on his arm. "I know," she said and went quiet.

The realization she no longer had a place to stay washed over her. *I don't have any extra money to stay somewhere else. I know they will need to give me my money back, but it probably won't happen for awhile. What am I going to do?*

In response to her silence, he said, "Before you say anything, hear me out. You can stay with me and Justin or I know Connie would welcome you in a heartbeat. Let us share the blessings God has given us. Grace, God put you and Connie together for a reason. I think one reason was so I could share my experience with you, but I think we are looking at another reason. We're your friends. Let us help. Here, let me call Joe and Connie."

She was inclined to say no, but really wasn't sure what other option she had. After a brief chat with Connie, Jeff handed the phone to Grace. Connie said, "Grace, as soon as they get your things, Jeff is going to bring you back here. We have loads of room and I want you to stay with us for the remainder of your stay in Hawaii. Joe really enjoyed your company tonight and would be happy to have you around during the days you want to hang out on the beach and I am at the restaurant. Please don't say no. So you see, I can do something for you and you can do something for me. Don't worry Grace. It's going to be okay."

"Thank you, Connie. I don't know what I was going to do. I cannot tell you what this means to me. You're a really good person. Thank you so much," and handed the phone back to Jeff.

He signed off with Connie and said, "Do you like the group MercyMe? Let me play a song for you from the album I mentioned earlier. Here, listen to the words."

As they listened to the song, the police officer waved at them and Jeff hopped out of the car to talk to his friend.

Listening to the remainder of the song, Grace was stunned at how these words were meant just for her. She knew God just reached out to her.

Staring at the flashing lights and emergency personnel, she thought about it. *In reality, what have I really lost here? I will eventually get my money back. I've made some really great friends who are going to help me out. Clearly God put them in my life for this very reason.*

She leaned to her side window to look up at the sky, smiled and said, "Okay, God. I see you are here. I am open to whatever you want to teach me through this hard time. I won't let it define me, but want to learn about how you define me. Let me see things your way. Thank you for Jeff and Connie and Joe."

Jeff opened the back and threw in her suitcases and a plastic bag of things the firefighters gathered up. It all stank of smoke. He got in the driver's seat and said, "They aren't sure much can be salvaged. Either smoke or water damaged everything, but they grabbed what they could see. How are you doing?"

Turning to look Jeff in the eye, her smile broke to a laugh and she said, "Jeff, I am good. I am really good. This will not define me. I am really okay."

Smiling at her, he patted her leg and said, "Awesome. Okay, let's get going." Nodding toward her ruined luggage, he said, "It stinks pretty badly. I'm afraid it might be ruined."

They drove back to Connie's and decided to leave the suitcases outside overnight to see if an airing would help.

Connie offered chamomile tea and the three of them stood around the kitchen talking. Grace opened her backpack. Thankfully, she had not had time to unpack it before coming for dinner. She pulled out her camera and tablet to find her phone. Jeff immediately commented on the camera saying he bought one like it, but was not really a good photographer. Seeing he was interested, Grace turned it on to let him look through the images.

Scrolling through slowly Jeff said, "Grace, these are really good. I really mean it. Being involved in advertising for the shops and promoting surfing events, I know good photography, and you are a natural. Have you sold any of your photographs?"

Stunned, Grace shook her head. She never thought much about it. She loved taking pictures and liked to have good prints on her walls, but never considered selling them.

"They're really good, Grace. You should think about selling them. I really like this one of this laughing kid, and this one of the sunrise, and these of the foam and waves. You have a really good eye. I'm glad your camera was in your backpack and here with you."

After they finished their tea, Jeff left and Connie settled Grace into a lovely spare room.

After she slipped into bed, she thought about what Jeff said and wondered if she could really sell her photos. Publishing would be pretty exciting and it could be a source of income. Rolling over, she silently thanked God for His provision in giving her a place to stay.

5 | The Simple Truth

October 21

The next morning Grace heard Connie head downstairs, so she got into her clothes from last night and met her in the kitchen. Connie was pulling out some fruit and yogurt for breakfast when Jeff came through the door. "Good morning, ladies! I could use a cup of coffee, if you don't mind, Connie. Grace, I stopped at the shop this morning and picked up a few things for you. I am afraid all your clothes are ruined," and he set a couple of bags on the counter.

Grace looked in and saw several T-shirts, shorts, a couple of bathing suits and flip-flops. "Oh Jeff, thank you. What do I owe you?"

"Nothing. I checked your size from the clothes in the suitcases out front before I left last night, so I am pretty sure these will fit, but if not, let me know."

Connie hugged Grace and said, "Jeff is always giving stuff away like this. I have a closetful. I wouldn't fight him on this. He considers it his mission to bless others from his abundance."

"Thank you, Jeff. You managed to get all colours I like. This is perfect

– all I need for my vacation."

"Well, not quite. One of the gals who works in my shop on weekends also works at the mall. She said she would pick up some underwear and a pair of jeans and drop them off today for you."

Grace looked up with tears in her eyes. Connie hugged her and told her she felt Grace filled a place in her heart left empty with Kim's passing.

Jeff reminded her of her promise to learn surfing that day and he would be back in the early afternoon. He thought the surf would be perfect for learning by then.

After Connie and Jeff left for work, Grace helped Joe clean up after breakfast. She gave her mom a call to update her then wandered out to the beach. She continued walking down the beach where she and Jeff had gone last night. She came across the place where they sat down to talk. Greenery and palm trees ringed a secluded spot with a beautiful view. Rather private and sheltered with a great view of the ocean. She could still see marks in the sand where they were sitting. She decided to take a break there to think over all the things that had happened in the last 12 hours.

She really should be more rattled, but felt at peace. As she considered this she realized she felt *at peace*. This shouldn't be, yet she felt really calm, unworried. A stillness quieted her heart and mind. She was okay.

As she considered her work circumstances, she was surprised at her tranquility. Right to her core, she was really okay. She leaned back in the sand, looking up at gently waving palm branches, and revelled in God's peace. *Oh God, you are here. Thank you so much for your peace, and in abundance.*

She lay there for quite awhile, resting in His peace. She wanted to enjoy this break in her stress. Her thinking hadn't changed, so clearly God filled her with His peace and rest.

She almost skipped back to Connie's house. She made lunch for Joe and herself, and helped him settle in the lanai for the afternoon. Apparently, he heard about the surf lessons and wanted to watch. Grace made sure he was aware of the other half of the deal.

Jeff arrived shortly after 1 p.m. with two of his surfboards and they headed down to the ocean. He looked at Grace and said, "Grace, you look happy. Something's changed, hasn't it?"

She smiled and said, "Yeah, I'm good. I am at peace and I am good. I cannot explain it, except to say this is God's peace in abundance and I feel at rest with things. So, surfer dude, what do I need to know to hang ten?"

Laughing, he informed her she would not be hanging ten today. They went through the basics and paddled out together. They floated for quite awhile as he taught her about reading the waves, when to start paddling and how to ride the wave in.

Despite the hard work Grace managed to stand and ride several waves in. She lost herself in the challenge and loved the time in the water. She would never forget this vacation. Already it was by far the best holiday she'd ever had.

They took a break, lying down on the boards, floating out past the breaking waves, and talked about surfing for awhile. Jeff complimented her on a good first day and encouraged her to keep practising. They talked about the huge winter waves that come into Waimea Bay. He said, "Standing on the beach when the big ones are rolling in gives you a real respect for the courage and skill of the few guys that go out to challenge nature and ride down the giant waves.

"Hey Grace, I have a great idea. Before the international riders arrive, we organize a surf competition, kind of an opener for the local guys and gals. We fit it in before the monster waves arrive in a couple of months, but it's still exciting. I sponsor the event. Would you mind coming this weekend to take some photos? You do such a great job of capturing people being natural, and maybe some shots showing the feel of the day and place? I could use them in promotions."

"Sure, if you really think I can give you something you don't already have."

"Yes, I think so. You have a good eye for catching the life within, the life of people, of nature, and the life of a place. I could pay you for the day."

"Oh Jeff, I am not a professional. How about I do this in exchange for all the clothes you have given me?"

"How about you spend the day taking photos and in exchange you get the few items of clothing, and in addition I pay you the standard rates for digital and print rights for all the ones I want to use for promotions? Deal?"

"Okay, deal." She wouldn't admit it to him, but she was a little excited. She looked forward to seeing her photos published. She needed to do a good job for him.

Jeff spotted Connie waving at them from the shore and waved back. "Looks like Connie's back. Are you getting hungry? You have more than met your half of our bargain. We can head in, if you like."

Grace said, "Couple more?"

He laughed. "You are hooked! Maybe I will see you riding in the competition on Saturday."

"Yeah, if they have a senior newbie category and little bunny waves."

They stayed out for another half hour before heading in. When they got to the lanai, Joe, Connie, Justin and about 15 to 20 people Grace didn't know were hanging out together. As soon as Jeff saw the crowd, he laughed. "Ah, I see. News travels very fast. I know why you are all here. I agreed to Joe and Connie, not everyone who works for me."

Grace was a little lost. She knew someone was up to a prank of some kind, but had no idea what it was about.

Jeff said, "Okay, Connie, Justin, which one of you organized the peanut gallery?" Both laughed, but denied their involvement.

Slowly, he turned to Joe and growled his name. "Joe. You are the only other person who knows everyone who works for me. I suspect the responsibility of this lies with you."

Joe, barely able to speak from laughing, put up his hands and said, "You got me, but I didn't twist anyone's arm to come. As soon as they heard you would be dancing, everyone dropped their plans. I understand they all brought their phones to gather blackmail evidence for future use."

Grace finally understood. She won the bargain, Jeff would be dancing on the beach, and Joe made sure there were plenty of amused watchers. She felt a little bad for Jeff. Especially if his dancing skill rivalled Elaine's from *Seinfeld* as everyone seemed to be expecting.

Jeff kicked up a bit of a fuss, but shot a quick wink in Grace's direction. She relaxed. He enjoyed the attention and made it fun for everyone. She hurried into her room to grab her camera. *May as well get in on the photo op.*

And Jeff delivered. He danced a wonderfully horrible dance on the beach while everyone hooted and encouraged ever-worsening dance moves. When sure everyone had photographed and videoed proof of his lack of talent, he turned and bowed to the crowd. In addition to the hoots he received, Grace could hear whistling and clapping from several houses down the beach.

Jeff really did enjoy life with no pretense. She knew he and Joe shared a solid relationship of trust and love. God truly blessed her when He brought her here. It occurred to her heaven would be like this, people having fun together, enjoying life, enjoying nature and enjoying each other. She didn't think she would get as close to heaven on earth as this moment – joy, fun, love, peace, good people and paradise to boot. It would be awesome in heaven, when she would no longer fight off the burdens of this world.

Everyone stayed for dinner and Jeff ordered Chinese food for the crowd. It turned into a party with all the young workers enjoying the company of their employer and his family. For a moment, she felt she really didn't belong there and intruded on something not hers to share.

Connie sat beside her. "Jeff really loves this kind of thing, making fun for everyone, especially those kids who work for him. They adore him. He never struggles to find employees. People line up to work in his shops. I continually learn a lot from him about managing people. He and Dad have been great mentors for me.

"I watched Jeff struggle after Kim's passing. They both attended church without fail, but he fell apart and totally disengaged from the world when she died. I really worried about him, but he found a peace and joy in God he never knew before. He says he has walked away from yesterday and tomorrow, and simply lives in this moment's grace.

"He's a new man. The kids love him and would follow him to the ends of the earth. He let go of carrying all the burdens of life, turning them over to Jesus, and now lives each day to the fullest in the freedom grace offers. As a result many of his employees found Christ. Yet, he is committed to a life where he dances in joy, loves, shares life, and leaves the burden of religion at the cross and the heavy lifting of worry and pain to God.

"I find inspiration in observing how he lives. I love coming back here because I love spending time with him. I lost my husband a year ago to a heart attack, and I count it a real gift to have seen the truth through the transformation in Jeff. I have followed him on the path of laying my burdens at the cross, and not picking them up again. I still miss my husband, but I am not lost in the grief. I simply choose not to put on the yoke of worry for tomorrow. God has totally blessed me with peace, freedom from the shackles and chains this corrupt life would like to lay on each of us.

"Grace, I am so happy throughout my being, living each day as it comes. All my debt was paid. God requires nothing more of me other than I accept His gift of life. Because He requires nothing more from me, I live freely every day as though I know the end of the story, because I do. And nothing I do will change the ending. I live in such a sweet release from the grip of life's burdens, I could dance every day, although I dance better than Jeff. Well, slightly better."

Smiling with a soft fondness, she continued. "Understanding the full truth of the completed work at the cross has turned my life on its head and I love looking at life from this perspective. In exchange for my complete trust in laying down my burdens, He gives abundant peace. My favourite verses are in the 4th chapter of Philippians. They say, 'Don't worry about anything; instead, pray about everything. Tell God what you need, and thank him for all he has done. Then you will experience God's peace, which exceeds anything we can understand. His peace will guard your hearts and minds as you live in Christ Jesus.' So I have taken Him at His word. I don't worry about anything, but pray and leave it with Him, and in exchange He fills me with peace. My heart sings and my mind is at rest. I will never go back to the old Christian life where I struggled daily and condemned myself for all my failings. My heart was heavy and guilt ridden, and my mind was stressed.

"I would have been devastated by the loss of my husband had it not been for Jeff. We talked almost daily. I know Jeff no longer strives to be a Christian leader, but continues to show many the path to true freedom in Christ. I think there are many who point to him as the witness who point-ed them to the truth of God's grace. He transformed into a beacon and magnet for many of us who were struggling. God uses him to share the simple truth of the cross with many of us desperate Christians."

The crowd of kids made for a fun and lively evening. Grace sat back and watched both Jeff and Connie, how they lived and loved despite the challenges in their lives. Grace wanted to have the same ease, peace and unstressed, loving presence in her life. She strove to be that kind of Chris-tian, but clearly never achieved it. She failed time and time again. But here, she watched the real thing – people dealing with pain and hurt in their lives, yet living at peace with themselves and the world around them. She wanted to know how to get an authentic worry-free life, not something put on for Sunday, but to really live it.

Jeff and Connie gave her a lot to think about. In bed that night she pulled out her Bible to read and decided on Galatians. The book Jeff said turned his world upside down. She prayed the Lord would remove any blindness or preconceptions and really show her the truth. She wanted His authentic peace, the worry-free way of life. She understood there would be challenges and difficulties in her life, but she wanted to walk in peace, not carrying the weight of the burdens these difficulties could bring.

Grace read through the familiar words slowly and carefully, to understand with a clear heart and mind. Christ obliterated religious rules and regulations, and the requirement to live under the law, when He declared, "It is finished." She wrote out her thoughts after reading the entire book. She wanted to remember and review these thoughts in the morning.

When she made the decision to let God be the God of her life, no further work or effort was required to live in peace and freedom. At the instant she turned to God and said, "I believe," she was made flawless. She thought she had understood it, but realized she thought it was a cleansing of the moment, and everything she did since repeatedly marked her with new black ugly stains of sin. But what she missed in decades of the Church she suddenly understood. At the moment she believed in the redemptive work of the cross, she was made flawless for all time. Christ paid the price for all sin of all time, not only what was in her past, but what would come in her future. No effort on her part could improve on flawless.

She marked in her Bible the cautionary verse, "You have been called to live in freedom…But don't use your freedom to satisfy your sinful nature. Instead, use your freedom to serve one another in love" (Galatians 5:13). That was exactly what she saw in both Connie and Jeff.

God called her to live in freedom. Now she understood what the cross really accomplished, and with no requirement to work to please God to earn His favour. But one thing remained unclear. *How was she to live in freedom?* Yawning, she rolled over. *I still need to figure out how Connie and Jeff do it.* With thoughts of living carefree, she fell into a deep, restful sleep.

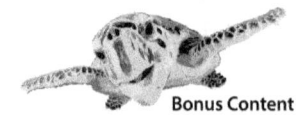

Bonus Content

Is there a place or thing that always grounds you? Do you have a favourite

place you go to get refreshed? Share your thoughts! Go to
www.serenitymclean.com/flawlessbonus/ and join the Inspiration Point
discussion.

The Flawless Life

6 | Hello, New Me

October 22

Grace awoke early the next morning before dawn and grabbed her tablet with her digital Bible. She quietly made her way to the lanai and walked down the beach to her spot in the sand sheltered by palms. This became her favourite spot – sheltered, private and surrounded by nature.

She reread Galatians. Something really caught her attention. Those who belong to Christ nailed their sinful nature (and worries) to the cross and let them die there. *Why would I try living my life by dragging these lifeless things around with me? They were nailed to the cross. Nailed. Permanently left in the hands of Christ and He carried them to the grave and left them there.*

She turned to Philippians to find the verse Connie had quoted. "Don't worry about anything; instead, pray about everything. Tell God what you need, and thank Him for all He has done. Then you will experience God's peace, which exceeds anything we can understand. His peace will guard your hearts and minds as you live in Christ Jesus" (Philippians 4:6–7).

Grace searched her tablet for passages on living in Jesus Christ, as she still remained confused. She tried to live for Him, but was met with daily failure. She turned to Ephesians and read, "Throw off your old sinful nature and your former way of life…Put on your new nature, created to be like God – truly righteous and holy" (Ephesians 4:22, 24).

Then she turned to 2 Corinthians to read, "So we have stopped evaluating others from a human point of view. At one time we thought of Christ merely from a human point of view. How differently we know Him now! This means anyone who belongs to Christ has become a new person. The old life is gone; a new life has begun! And all of this is a gift from God, who brought us back to himself through Christ. And God has given us this task of reconciling people to him. For God was in Christ, reconciling the world to himself, no longer counting people's sins against them" (2 Corinthians 5:16–19).

This led her to Galatians where she read, "My old self has been crucified with Christ. It is no longer I who live, but Christ lives in me. So I live in this earthly body by trusting in the Son of God, who loved me and gave himself for me."

Could it be? Christ created a new spirit, a new life within her she never really understood? Is it this new life God sees? A shiny new life made truly and permanently righteous and holy? The old one was left hanging on the cross?

If that's the case, if this new life lives within, and the old one is dying daily in sin – but – so, God only sees me as this new being?

That's it. Grace moaned at the impact of her realization. All these years, and she never understood. Not only were her sins of the day wiped away the day she believed, but God wiped out *all* of her sin of past, present and future. He sees none of the sins of her sinful nature because all sin was wiped away for all time and left hanging on the cross. She was no longer an old dying thing, but a shiny new life.

She was this shiny new creature, made flawless and is flawless forever. She didn't need to earn God's pleasure to be worthy of His love and attention. He couldn't love her any more and requires nothing more from her.

Well, that seems incredible and so easy. I can pray about my needs and worries, leave it with Him and live in the peace I see in Connie and Jeff.

That was the key she was searching for. Because she was made flawless, there was no pressure on her, ever. In her flawless state God carried her in His full care. She warranted and received His full attention at all times. She now lived as His beloved and He remained pleased with her as is. She did not need to strive through failing human effort to be any better.

Now she simply needed to live her life accepting her flawless state. She needed to leave it all, all the worry, all the stress, all the financial responsibilities, all of her future in His hands and live in His freedom and peace. She was flawless and cherished.

Grace prayed about her future and her financial needs. She told God what she needed, thanked Him for all He had done. She picked up a couple of pebbles and walked to the ocean. She took the first one and said, "This is my worry about a job," and threw it as hard as she could into the surf. She took the second pebble and said, "This is my financial responsibilities," and threw it as well. She finished by saying, "Lord, I give my need for a job and my financial responsibilities into your hands. I leave my worries in your living water. They will never rise to the surface again. I commit to leaving them buried in your ocean."

Grace felt the chains slowly releasing. Worry washed away in waves of peace. Her heart exploded in the joy of the freedom from the burden of her future.

The sun began to rise over the ocean's horizon and she realized a new day dawned in her spirit, in her heart and mind. She now looked at things through the eyes of her new creature. And the view was fantastic.

It really didn't matter what this world put in her path, whether a lost job or a lost place to stay, she remained flawless and beloved. Her future safely resided in the hands of the Almighty. She lived worthy of His care, love and attention. Nothing more was required than to accept and stay in His peace.

She no longer focused on the stresses of life. They could not pull her out of His caring hands, His protection, His provision, so why worry?

With a deep breath, she looked over the breadth of the sky and danced through the water's edge on her way back to the house. She could take each day as it came and simply leave the rest to the Lord. She could live her life as though she were flawless – because God made her flawless for all time.

With all her burdens tossed into the ocean, Grace left behind the crushing, life-sucking worry, and her slavery to trying various things to earn God's care and attention. She felt a thousand pounds lighter. Just because she didn't see or "have" the solution to her lack of a job, well, the responsibility of provider no longer resided with her and she would not pick up those burdens again. It all belonged to the Creator of the universe. Unlike the tsunami of self-pity that left her desolate, and not any lighter of her burdens, she experienced an authentic release of her worry and joy instead of emptiness.

And then a foundational truth hit her. God's plan and provision for her life would best anything she could come up with. She only needed to believe she now existed in a flawless state, loved, cherished and prized. No need to worry about her future. Everything lay in God's hands. Nothing but rest was required of her. Absolutely stunning. The path was made so easy. Trust and rest. Really?!

Then she understood.

That means what I thought was God's silence was not His silence at all. God already put provision in my path. Just because I cannot see into tomorrow, I know the creator of all took care of it long ago. It is finished, already done. I didn't need to plead and beg Him to action. No, He already provided, it is finished. And He requires no circus of performance from me – just trust and faith. All the chaos and stress, all my failed effort – not required? What a relief!

This was stunning.

Wait – resting in trust and faith may sound easy, but I can see some problems. Knowing myself, the challenge, as with many biblical people, will be to not become an Abraham. Best to not interfere with God's yet unseen provision in a vain human attempt to make it happen through my own strength. She thought about the pain down through the ages as a result of Abraham "helping" God in producing a son through Hagar.

She looked back to the place where she had thrown the pebbles in to remind herself she would never pick them up again. His peace flooded through her and she knew all would be okay, even though she could not see how. Peace engulfed her, and she danced in the freedom from her burdens. She knew God fulfilled His promise of peace and it exceeded her understanding.

That afternoon Grace swam out past the breaking waves. She wanted to feel the ocean wrap around her without being tossed about in the churning surf. She became totally lost in the delightful feel of the warm water running through her hair and washing over her skin as she repeatedly dove underwater and swam as far as she could. She was captivated by the sense of weightless freedom, yet fully supported. She was not standing on ground, but wrapped in water – she could not fall. This physical sensation was exactly how she felt in her soul. Floating, light, weightless, yet fully supported and protected. And she wanted to relive the sensation over and over again, to embed it permanently in her memory.

Tired, she floated on the surface, utterly happy. She looked up to see where she was and noted she was drifting south down the coast. Then she sensed something huge dark coming underneath her from behind.

Terror filled her mind and seized her heart. *It can't be.* But something big loomed underneath. *How close? Can I swim for shore? Can I poke out its eye? Okay, I have to be brave and look the predator square on. Face the enemy. Oh God, stand with me.*

With bile rising to her throat, she bravely looked down between her feet to deal with the impending shark attack. And instantly the tension left her body. The fear receded.

A giant sea turtle gently swam underneath her through the bay. He moved in graceful, easy strokes. Grace took a breath and tried to keep up with him. Even though she was a strong swimmer, without fins she couldn't do it. She swam her hardest to keep him in sight as long as she could, but he disappeared into the distant water.

What a marker for a life-changing day. She never forgot it, the day she understood flawless. Deep, scary things may come upon her, but they were really just turtles. She had nothing to worry about, knowing she rested in the hands of the Almighty who would protect her and take care of her needs. That was His job. Hers was to trust she was made flawless and therefore beloved beyond measure. Yes, this world would drop its cares in her path, but she didn't need to pick them up. She needed to turn them over to God.

Grace swam for shore and headed back, walking along in the shallows, occasionally kicking up a spray of water and laughing. She knew God had renewed her mind, given her a whole new perspective on her life on earth.

When she got back to the house, she prepared dinner for Joe, Connie and herself. After dinner Connie returned to the restaurant to work with the evening shift. Joe and Grace spent the evening on the lanai with a neighbour who had dropped in, and then she headed for bed early. Tomorrow she would go to the surf competition and wanted a good night's sleep as they had planned a very early start.

October 23

Jeff picked her up along with several others going to the event as the sun was peaking over the ocean's horizon.

They arrived early at Waimea Bay and several got busy setting up for the competition. Grace wandered the length of the park and beach to get a feel for the place. It gradually filled up with a wide variety of people from young toddlers to old retired men, and surfer guys and gals to banker types. She took a number of pictures of people interacting with the area in some way – playing in the sand, surfer rituals, toes in the water, studied faces watching the surf grow, signing in, and what Grace guessed was the usual strutting and boasting which goes with this type of competition.

Jeff said the waves were not too big today, but to her eyes they were plenty big. For awhile, she stood in the surf at the water's edge and took some shots of those heading out, and several of a young couple with an 18-month-old toddler. They hung out in the light wash of the waves with the toddler sitting on a board, giggling with every rush of a wave. She got several shots of this young lad's anticipation of the next one, and the burst of joy and delight as each and every one came.

Grace found the actual competition quite spectacular to watch, having recently learned to surf in itty bitty waves compared to what these brave folks were riding. She marvelled at the age range of athletes. Some seemed pretty old, but still really skilled surfers.

Everyone enjoyed a fun day, and as they drove home conversation centred around the day's events. Grace let her thoughts wander through what she found interesting and came back to the toddler on the board.

This is really what she should be like, living in the freedom of the moment, laughing through life without a care in the world. Her Father had his hand on her board, making life fun and exciting, but not taking her into dangerous waters. She needed to laugh and enjoy the moment, and delight in the anticipation of the next exciting wave.

The more she thought about the little boy the more she thought this is much like what her life should be like. Her past was past. This young lad accepted his parents without a thought. He did nothing to earn their devotion, attention and care. He simply existed as their child and that was enough.

God's hand always remained on her surfboard, bringing her to a new experience. By thinking she needed to earn His favour, she ignored the fact the cross was enough. Trying to rebuild the old system of works Christ had torn down was disregarding His completed work.

Like Abraham, God counted her fully righteous simply because of her faith. And she could walk through life in freedom because she believed in Jesus.

It was quite a concept, really too good to be true. Just leave all your worry with God, and in exchange be filled with peace. Just sit on the surfboard and giggle with every wave. With all her life's worry and stress, resting on the surfboard sounded pretty good.

7 | Giggling on the Surfboard

October 24

The next morning, Jeff picked up Connie and Grace to go to the church in Kaneohe only to find JD Farag had left for the mainland for several weeks of teaching and vacation. A local man spoke instead. While the message interested Grace, she felt disappointed to not meet JD.

After lunch Grace downloaded all the images to Jeff's laptop. They spent the next hours poring over them and picking out what he wanted to purchase as professional shots. They agreed on four to be made into posters, three for promotional purposes, and one to use as graphics on T-shirts. For full rights, for ten years, he offered $25,000 and a royalty on all sold items, which he estimated to be about $20,000 over the next two years.

Shocked at his offer, both Jeff and Joe assured her he offered a fair deal. He emailed her a contract with the details and encouraged her to get some independent advice. She forwarded it to a friend in marketing to ask their opinion. She didn't want Jeff's pity or charity, and wanted to be sure the deal was actually fair for him.

After dinner, Grace called her mom to let her know all was well and to check that she was okay. Connie and Grace settled in to enjoy the sunset when they heard a loud crash followed by a painful yell. They ran to check on Joe. He had fallen in the bathroom and needed their help to get back up. Once upright, Joe realized the fall further damaged the already broken bone in his leg. They helped him out to the car and took him to the emergency department of the local medical centre.

They waited for new x-rays which showed the fall twisted the bone, fracturing it into three pieces. The extensive damage would require surgery. The hospital admitted Joe and gave him some painkillers for the night, with surgery scheduled for the next day.

October 25

Connie left early the next morning to stop in and see her dad, then head to the restaurant. In the evening after visiting Joe, she said the surgery went well and that he was resting quietly with the painkillers.

Grace enjoyed her day on the beach and prepared a cold dinner so it would be ready whenever Connie came home. They enjoyed their chicken caesar salad on the lanai, listening to the rhythmical sound of the waves.

After dinner Connie said, "Grace, I have a bookshop along the waterfront back home. The owner of the restaurant next to mine put it up for sale and I have bought the space. I want to knock the wall out and open the space as a coffee shop and a comfortable place to hang out and read. I have all the permits, and I have the contractors lined up. I planned on being back in time for all the work, but with dad's surgery, I think he really needs me down here longer than I had anticipated, at least until he gets back on his feet at work. What would you think about taking on the opening of the coffee shop as a project? I could really use someone I can trust to look after things there while I am here. If this work is not done now, I will be waiting for months to get all the workers lined up again. I don't mean to put you on the spot, but would you think about it and let me know? It would be a huge favour to me and to Joe as well."

"Are you sure? I've never managed facilities or construction projects."

"I'm absolutely sure. Watching you handle all this stress in your life with strength, I know you walk with God. Combined with experience managing plans, schedules and people, I know I couldn't find anyone better to take care of things there for me."

Indeed, she thought about it. It sounded like a great opportunity, but she wanted to be sure she could do a good job. While she researched what goes into a renovation plan, she heard from her marketing friend. He looked at the eight images, combed through the contract, and confirmed Jeff's assessment of the images and that the contract detailed a fair deal for both parties.

In bed Grace began to really think through what occurred in the last week. The week started with a feeling God remained distant and not attending her desperate need. Life ate her up and spat her out as a big failure. A cold, broken woman boarded the plane, reluctantly engaging with this world that had steamrolled over her.

But all along, even before she had bought the tickets months ago, God had given her the desire to come to Hawaii on vacation. She couldn't foresee His plans to confront her misunderstandings, to bring her to the freedom and easy yoke He had promised, and to open new doors. All along He ensured His provision waited for her. While she cried her heart out, letting the emotional waves crash over her, allowing fear and terror to rule her thoughts, this opportunity anticipated her arrival.

And then it occurred to Grace that "It is finished" included His provision at this very moment. What a profound thought! So profound, she sat up. Her legs became suddenly restless and she felt excitement building in her stomach.

She got out of bed and threw on some shorts. She needed to get out to the beach.

Well after midnight, the beach relaxed in the quiet and darkness. Countless stars sprayed across the heavens. She started toward her spot, but instead walked into the ocean. She wanted to feel the water washing over her legs, the place she tossed her cares.

She raised her arms to her King, with tears pouring down her cheeks. All she could utter was, "Thank you, thank you, thank you." After an unmeasured time, a light breeze brushed her cheek, bringing her back to an awareness of time and place. With a heart full of comfort and satisfaction, she caught a scent of sweetness, not of flowers or perfume, and knew she was standing in the presence of the Almighty.

She really thanked her beloved Lord for guiding her path and putting her in this place. He promised to consistently provide for her needs, period. Whether she rested or stressed made no difference. He said she only needed to pray and rest in trust.

She slowly and quietly made her way back along the beach and into her bed. She understood this peace came not from the provision, but from knowing He held all of her tomorrows in His hand, and even if she couldn't see the answer, He always provided. Resting or worrying made no difference. He planned and provided even before trouble arose. It truly was finished. The work, worry, provision and path of her life was completed at the cross.

October 26

When Grace finally awoke the next morning, she put in a quick call to her mom then grabbed her tablet and skipped down the beach. After thanking God for making a way for her to live life in peace and freedom from worry, she started to think about Connie's proposal to take on the café project. She made several notes, mostly questions to go through with Connie before agreeing to managing the construction.

She grabbed a lunch of fruit and took one of the old surfboards out to spend the afternoon on the water. She managed to catch a few good waves and was quite pleased with herself.

Resting out past the breaking waves, she thought trust was easy right now as she was on an emotional high, but she needed to remember to not take on worry about her tomorrows, but trust God already provided, with more in store. Like that little toddler, she needed to sit on the surfboard and giggle with each wave.

She now understood when Jesus said, "I tell you the truth, unless you turn from your sins and become like little children, you will never get into the Kingdom of heaven." She needed to forget looking at life from her analytical, earthly eyes, because He's God of the unseen and God of the impossible. *Sit and rest on the surfboard. Take delight in every rush of water under my board.*

Connie spent the evening with Joe at the hospital. His recovery progressed without complication after his surgery and he would be coming home in a couple of days.

Jeff arrived as Grace prepared a light supper for herself. He invited her out for a seafood dinner and she readily agreed. On the way, she chatted about her bravery and fantastic surfing skill at riding the ginormous 4 ft. waves.

Over dinner they discussed Connie's project. She knew his experience offered sound advice. She laid out her concerns and he challenged her thinking, causing her to reframe her thoughts. He offered one obvious comment which simplified her concerns. "You worry you will authorize something Connie won't be happy with, so what prevents you from working with Connie as you would with any other sponsor, leaving the big decisions to her?"

She thought about it and admitted if they established boundaries, sponsor and project manager responsibilities, and regular meetings over Skype, she could manage this as any other project.

October 28

Joe came home the next evening. He was doing remarkably well after surgery, but tired quickly. Over dinner, the three talked through the proposal for Grace to manage the construction project and for Connie to stay on longer to help Joe.

Joe enthusiastically supported the idea. He had appreciated Connie's help over the last week and felt relieved for her to extend her stay. He eagerly wanted to get back to work, but after his fall he realized he best not push his recovery. He gratefully thanked both women for their proposal.

The construction started in four weeks. Connie suggested Grace extend her stay in Hawaii for an extra couple of weeks to spend their evenings planning. A couple of weeks of preparation would give a good foundation for Grace to head up the project in Connie's absence. They agreed on a consulting rate fair to both of them.

When Connie and Joe had gone to bed, Grace headed out to the beach. She went to her spot and lay with her arms behind her head, looking up at a star-filled sky. *Another three weeks in paradise. Oh God, you are good.* She considered the scale and size of the universe. All these giant celestial bodies were in His hands as He directed their paths. The Bible says He stretches out the heavens like a canopy and spreads it out like a tent to live in. Amazing. She pondered if, when the Christians are raptured, this universe would be their playground. And what amazing things would they discover?

And then to think the One who created and is in control of the entire universe cherished her enough to ensure all her needs were taken care of. This could be hard to believe. But she must not forget – He created in her a new creature. A flawless and unblemished eternal spirit being He loved beyond all He had created in His universe. This is where she needed to live spiritually and mentally.

As the Bible instructed, she had thrown off her old sinful nature and put on her new nature, which was created to be righteous and holy. Her job now was to let the Holy Spirit renew her thoughts and attitudes to align with this new righteous and holy creature, rather than drag old dead thoughts and attitudes to taint her fresh new view of life through heaven's eyes. And what a difference this change in view made to her confidence and trust in His care for her. Nothing visible had changed, but her whole perspective of Christian life had changed from stress and failure to a focus on heaven, and a disregard for the worry and stress with which life's issues would like to bog her down.

End of October, Early November

Her late night visits to this private beach spot became a regular practice for the remainder of her time in Hawaii. Through her time there with her Maker, her faith and trust grew in strength and became fixed in her heart and mind. He had taken her away from her familiar life to breathe His refreshing, healing breath into her new creature. She had never felt so alive. And every night she thanked Him for His life in her.

Joe was improving with each day. Grace enjoyed spending time with him in the mornings as she prepared for her meetings with Connie in the evening and spent her afternoons on the beach. The work settled her into the familiar and comforting rhythm of a project. When it was time for Grace to return home, she was confident in the state of the project and felt ready to get to the store.

Emma, a semiretired accountant and Connie's friend, managed the store while Connie was away. Grace spoke with Emma a couple of times over the phone. She pictured a sweet, kind, grandmotherly type and looked forward to working with her.

Jeff offered to drive Grace to the airport and she happily took him up on his offer. She wanted to get any last minute advice he could offer.

After they talked over her concerns of working with the contractors, she asked a question itching at her mind. "Jeff, why do you always say Yehovah instead of God and Yeshua instead of Jesus? Is it a messianic thing?"

Laughing he said, "No, nothing religious. When I came to understand I was a new, flawless being, I felt I stepped into a new way of relating to Yehovah and really wanted to keep the new relationship at the forefront of my heart and mind. You know, God is a title, but Yehovah is His name. I decided if I am going to trust Him with all my tomorrows, I should call Him by His name. It reminds me of the life-changing view of being a new creature. I do not wish to go back to my old ways. I am totally committed to this new life. I think of Yehovah and Yeshua in a whole new way, and by using these names I bring intimacy to my consciousness."

Jeff proved an interesting person and she loved the way he thought about life, and how he walked his own path and didn't care if he was different. He loved, he cared about those around him, but lived his life in such an authentic way. He was following the God of the impossible, doing things in each of their lives in crazy, unpredictable and wildly new ways, only asking for their trust.

She hoped she could be equally authentic in her walk with – Yehovah. She liked this switch to using God's name, although it would take time to make the change. She liked the way it came out so naturally for Jeff and how it spoke of his close relationship with his saviour.

8 | Return to Reality

November 9

The day after returning home, Grace headed out early to the bookstore. Construction started in a couple of weeks. She wanted to spend some time with Emma and follow up with all the contractors, confirming they were still committed to the timeline.

Emma personified grandmotherly as she expected and loved her from the first moment. She managed the bookstore successfully, but developed concerns about taking on the task of managing the construction. She gratefully welcomed Grace, ready to manage all the work, the contractors, the permits and inspections. Emma loved Connie and would have done it, but it was a great relief to see Grace onboard.

She also met Brigit, the young gal who worked full-time for Connie. Grace watched Brigit and Emma together and noted the kind, respectful way Brigit treated Emma. She decided quickly she liked this young woman.

Grace enjoyed spending time at the bookstore. Located on Cordova Bay Road in Victoria, near the golf course and right on the waterfront, it offered comfortable seating with big windows across the ocean side, and a great view of the Haro Strait. Floor-to-ceiling window sliders opening to a small but beautiful outdoor café area graced the other half of the building. Grace thought this would act as a great venue for book readings, book clubs and other artistic gatherings.

The Indian summer day enticed Grace to settle at one of the outdoor café tables. Although closed, the path from the side still granted access to the outdoor section. Over the span of a few hours, the tables gradually filled up. Some folks brought a coffee from elsewhere and enjoyed the day and the view, while others met friends and colleagues. Clearly the regulars favoured this haunt.

Grace worked intently on her laptop when a tall middle-aged man approached and asked if she minded sharing her table. She briefly glanced around, noting the other tables were filled. She smiled and invited him to sit, making room for his tablet and coffee.

He took in a deep breath, looking over the water and said, "What a great day. It almost feels like spring."

Grace half closed her laptop, and looked out over the deep blue of the water and sky. She couldn't imagine living far from the ocean. She loved days of sun-soaked, linen-fresh ocean air. Turning to this stranger, she said, "This is my favourite kind of day and I couldn't resist spending time out here. Do you come here regularly?"

Laughing, he said, "You could say that. I used to own this restaurant and spontaneously put it up for sale. I think I was curious as to what it was worth, and then it sold more quickly than I expected. And now I find I am without work. I am Kevin Davis, by the way."

Grace said, "Grace McConnell." She shook his hand. Curious, she asked, "Are you looking to stay in the restaurant and service industry? Or are you looking for a real change?"

Kevin leaned back, settling into his chair, and looked out into the distance. After a pause he looked Grace in the eye and said, "You know, you are the first to ask me this question. I hadn't even asked it of myself."

He paused, looked back out over the ocean, and Grace watched his lips purse, brows come together and eyes slightly squint. "I like the question. You make me think –"

Grace let the pause rest comfortably between them as Kevin drifted in thought. Finally he said, "I think the truth is I want to do something new and different. The restaurant business runs in my family. I never considered that by selling my business, new doors to something entirely different would open. I'm not sure what lies behind them. It all happened more quickly than expected. I believed I could take my time to figure it out. So here I sit to ponder my future."

They chatted on about the restaurant, the reno project for Connie, and how they both loved living in Victoria. After half an hour of companionable conversation, Kevin left for an appointment and Grace carried on with her work.

The evening equalled the day, and warmth lingered in the air. Grace took her golden retriever Abbey for a walk along the beach. Abbey always loved a walk, but was ecstatic about visiting the ocean. Grace would ask, "Want to go to the beach?" and Abbey would race to the door, giving an excited bark. If she was not quick enough, Abbey would race from the door to her and back to the door, barking excitedly. She loved the beach.

She took time while Abbey was off sniffing the shoreline to pray about everything of the day, telling Yehovah what she needed and thanking Him for all He had done. Out along the waterfront, away from people, alone with nature and her best girl, she found renewed peace about her future. Her heart and mind rested.

She filled with a quiet, settled joy about living her days focused on the immediate path before her, and she left tomorrow's worries to the One who cherished her and wanted to be her provider.

She determined to stay in her bubble of trust and peace, regardless of what came along. Her work lay in resisting her inclination to pick up the burden of worry – daily. She prayed about her needs, gave thanks, and then rested in the understanding she was flawless in His eyes, a being He wanted to shower with love and provision.

They both returned home full of happy.

9 | Unseen Provision

November 12

Several busy days later while in the back of the bookstore on the phone with one of the contractors, Brigit came back with a note for her. Glancing at the note Grace mouthed, "Give me five minutes." Brigit nodded and returned to the storefront.

After hanging up, she reread the message.

Kevin Davis is asking to speak with you.

Kevin Davis? Is he one of the contractors? She headed to the front, a little worried she had forgotten someone or something. As she rounded the corner, Kevin approached her with two large Starbucks cups, offering her one. He said, "I understand chai is your weakness. Care to join me for a break?"

She accepted the cup. "Sure. How did you know I love chai latte?"

Winking at Brigit he said, "I have my ways." And she realized Brigit probably knew Kevin quite well, having worked beside his restaurant. "Would you like to sit inside or outside?" She thought it was a bit too chilly for her today and indicated inside. He headed to the back of the bookstore and chose a couple of chairs near the windows, offering a bit of privacy.

"I wanted to thank you for our conversation the other day. It probably seems like a minor thing to you, but your question really made me think and I have been thinking nonstop since about the open door before me. I had blinders on, only considering more of the same for my future. But you made me realize a world of possibility exists. So –", raising his cup to Grace's, "thank you for giving me the world."

Laughing she said, "You're welcome, but I didn't give you the world. It was always there."

"Ah, but you blew out the walls and now I see it. It's like a huge menu. I'm having trouble figuring out what I want."

"What do you enjoy doing in your spare time?"

"Oh, well, I love sailing and spend a lot of time on the water. And I enjoy spending time with my two nephews. Eric's my sister's son and Shane's my brother's son."

His soft smile slid to concern. "Eric's a smart lad, but is really struggling since his father was in a car accident and left in a coma. They pulled the plug on life support a few months back. He and his dad were very close and he's devastated."

"Is he in high school?"

"No, he's on the cusp of dropping out of his first year of engineering at university. It's hard to watch such a promising young man crumble apart."

"I'm sorry. It's sad he's having such a tough time. Do you see much of him?"

"Only on holidays. He's in school in Ontario."

"Is he coming home for the Christmas break?"

"Yes." He took in a breath, raised his finger and wagged it in the air, looking at Grace for a long moment. "You know, Eric loves sailing. I should get the boat fitted out for an extended sail and take him up through the islands."

"Just for fun? Or are you thinking something more?"

He tilted his head and looked at Grace intently. Squinting, he said,

"Hmm, what do you mean 'something more'?"

She shrugged slightly. "I don't know. Just wondering if you thought a just fun, 'be there,' buddies kind of trip. You know, sail hard all day and kick back and play in the evening, or if you thought to get Eric away from distractions to discuss some potentially difficult topics."

He pursed his lips. Grace turned to watch a heavy-laden cargo ship making its way south.

After a long while he said, "At first I thought to keep it casual and fun and let things play out how they will, but Eric deserves so much more than leaving it to chance that we talk through the things bringing him down. And I really should prepare myself to handle whatever we get into."

Although he faced the ocean, he was alone with his thoughts. She remained quiet and waited.

"I believe the value of taking him sailing lies in more than a distraction. This could be life changing for him. I have a counsellor friend I will ask for advice to prepare. I want Eric to say 20 years from now, 'Uncle Kevin changed my perspective and my life.' How incredible to play a part in transforming a young man's life! As I think about it, I need to focus my time and attention on helping him."

Finally looking at Grace he said, "No 'be a buddy' for me. No, I see an opportunity to mentor Eric. Thank you again, Grace. You've scored two for two now. You really make me think."

Then smiling he said, "I would like to book a session with you every week. Maybe I can figure out what to do with my future."

The Flawless Life

10 | Walking in Flawless

Remainder of the Year to Early January

Grace thought Kevin was joking about coming to chat, but he stopped in regularly to share a coffee break and talk about a variety of things he'd been thinking about. They fell into a comfortable routine. Kevin shared where he was at in his plans and she asked questions to prompt his thinking and spark his imagination.

In the meantime the construction progressed at a good pace. Grace spoke almost daily with Connie via Skype, often walking around with her tablet, giving Connie a view of the progress. They discussed Connie's satisfaction at the renovations and the slow progress of Joe's recovery. They agreed to extend Grace's contract for another three months to complete all the construction, finishing and furnishing work.

She saw increasingly less of Kevin as Christmas approached, and nothing of him during the holidays. Then on New Year's Day she received an email invite to dinner the following weekend. She readily accepted, excited to hear how the sailing and mentoring trip had gone.

She asked where they would dine, but he limited the information to,

"The restaurant offers casual dining." He picked her up and they headed downtown to Olo, a downtown contemporary, bright and warm fine dining restaurant featuring Northwest cuisine.

They chatted about renovations, the project extension and about her Christmas. She told him the contractors and their employees took a week off over Christmas, and she spent time down at the ocean with her golden retriever.

Their conversation about Grace had taken them through to the break between appetizer and entrée. She said, "So – don't leave me in suspense any longer. How did it go with Eric?"

With a big grin he said, "Well, you know I have a counsellor friend? I spent some time with her getting information on how I could help him. And I spent some time with my sister to get her read on how he was doing. And then I thought about how I wanted to approach him. And I prepared things to do conducive to talking. I was all ready for the trip.

"Then Eric showed up with his buddy from university and I thought all my plans were for naught. Eric seemed to not care whether we went or not, but his friend Andrew was pretty keen. Andrew comes from Taiwan, and planned to stay at the university over the holidays rather than go back home.

"I think Eric agreed to go sailing to avoid dealing with the pain and emotion at home. And I think avoidance explained why he brought Andrew along.

"I still tried to execute on my plans with Eric even with Andrew there. The first day brought a stiff wind making for an exciting sail, but he stayed pretty aloof. That evening I felt the trip would fail to achieve all I hoped. But while on deck watching the sun set, I thought about things, about the times you and I talked things through. I really analyzed what you do to expand my narrow thinking to worlds of opportunity. And I revised my plans.

"The next day while Eric was at the helm, he said, 'I always thought sailing would be boring, but this is kind of fun, and I saw a crack in his wall. I asked if the two guys would like to learn the basics of being crew and helmsman. Andrew, always the more enthusiastic, readily agreed. Eric, still reserved, gave me a shrug and a 'Sure,' but I could see the engineer was intrigued.

"We took a long midday break and pulled out the charts. I gave them some basic instructions on how to plot a course and left the two engineers for the next couple of hours to plot out the remainder of our trip. I heard them negotiating with each other as they worked. They asked a few questions, predominantly about where they could see various things, but for the most part I left it to them to figure it out.

"Eric started to show his leadership when they came to discuss the route. He presented a compelling argument for tackling a difficult passage.

"I planned a sailing lesson of some sort each day. We talked well into the evenings about the day's sail, but then conversation drifted to life, future and their plans. Then I implemented the Grace technique.

"I asked questions. At first, Eric didn't respond. But out on the ocean, away from daily routine, he let go of his wall of silence. I watched the real Eric awaken and rise up.

"Over the days our relationship tightened in trust. We eventually dove into some really deep and meaningful conversations about his challenge with his dad's passing. I stuck with the Grace technique and he kept coming back for more conversation. Just like me with you.

"I really thank you, Grace. I benefitted from you, both in gaining clarity in my own thinking, and in reaching Eric. We made plans to go back out on another trip this spring when he finishes his year."

She watched Kevin as he spoke of his trip, and his success with Eric and his satisfaction, his pleasure, his happiness. She said, "I think I see your passion."

Nodding slowly he said, "Yeah, I'll never forget my week with Eric. I –." He snapped his attention to Grace and pursed his lips. His gaze dropped to the table, no longer looking at anything, but lost in thought.

After a long moment, he looked back at her and said, "You know, I really enjoyed spending time with Eric, investing in him, to actually contribute in a meaningful way to his life. I've never done anything like this before. I spent my time focused on my restaurant. You're right, Grace. This is a passion I would like to explore more."

"How do you see this passion? As a sideline? Or is it something you see as a full-time thing?"

Their meal arrived and while they dealt with drinks refreshed and ground pepper, he had a couple of minutes to think.

"I wonder what it would look like if I did something like this full-time? I'm not prepared to get a counselling degree, but something that allows me to help others."

"Well, what aspects of the trip really resonate? What do you see as the pieces you feel most passionate about? What really satisfies you to the core?"

"The whole thing. I loved spending time teaching the knowledge and skills of sailing, I loved the camaraderie of 'the boys,' and I really loved the deep conversations, watching their thoughts fill with possibility and finishing with two transformed lives."

"So why not do the same thing for others?"

He dropped his utensils, sat back in his chair and stared at her. Leaning forward he emphatically pointed at her and said, "That's it! That is it! Oh, this is fantastic! I could take out all kinds of people. Businessmen looking for inspiration, men beaten down in life, struggling divorcées, young entrepreneurs, there's many possibilities!"

He stood up, leaned over the table and kissed Grace on the cheek. "Thank you so much. I think this is my thing. You did it again. This is what I want to do for others. Thank you so much.

"Say," he said, "how would you like to go out for a weekend on the boat? Bring a friend, if you like. I would like to treat you to time on the water. Nothing in the world like it. I can teach you about sailing, if you would like to learn."

The next weekend Kevin, Grace and her best friend went out for a couple days' sail. She relished the time learning about how a sailboat works, crewing for Kevin, and she loved the feel of the helm under a stiff wind, racing across the waves. She understood why he loved being out on the water so much.

In the middle of the night she awoke with a gasp, pulled to her consciousness from a deep dream. She sat up for a moment, then quietly slipped out of the bunk bed, got dressed and went to the galley, closing the door behind her. She quietly made herself a hot chocolate and stretched out on the sofa to think about her astounding dream.

Looking down on earth from high in the sky, she saw the entire earth shudder as though a shiver went down its spine. And the shaking caused death and distress for people around the world. But she was holding hands with a line of Hawaiian people and they remained unharmed and survived the disaster. It felt so real, she knew this dream had significance, but many years would pass before she discovered the meaning.

She heard a noise as someone made their way to the head and a few minutes later stepped into the galley. Kevin spotted her, sat down beside her and asked if she was okay. After a bit of chatter, he paused and said, "Grace, I've wanted to ask you something for awhile." Looking down at his hands he said, "I've watched you now over a couple of months. Regardless of what is going on with the contractors, you remain at ease. So peaceful. You impacted my life in significant ways already. And I look forward to the time I spend with you. Your peace rubs off on me and I spend the rest of my day elevated. For weeks, I tried to figure out what you do to surround yourself in calm and cannot figure it out."

Looking back at her he said, "I would like to know your secret. Is it a way of thinking or what? Whatever it is, I want to know."

She sat without words for a moment. For the first time in her entire life someone asked about the source of the "fruit" of her life. She quickly prayed she would say the right thing, the right way, and the Spirit would open Kevin's eyes to the truth of what she would share.

Grace honestly shared the good and bad of her journey to peace, her story of losing her job, the trip to Hawaii, and what she had learned about the real meaning of what Yeshua had done on the cross. She shared the pain of her struggles with fear and the difference now, about the peace when she prays about her needs, and how she leaves all her worries with Yehovah. She told him she lived in a mess of emotion tossed about by the inevitable storms of life, but now she lived a steady, restful life.

She remembered something she recently read in a blog by Nickolas Hiemstra. She shared her favourite quote. "'Oh, I am not saying they [the believers] will not experience times of trial and testing, but those times will not be times of crisis, but mere challenges to their fleshly desires and comfort. No big deal, little "blips" on the screen.' And this is really where I am living out my life. The storms of fear and terror are now no big deal, just little blips on my journey."

When she finished, Kevin remained quiet for a long while, then thanked her for sharing such a personal story. He stood up and said he wanted to spend some time thinking, but would come back to this conversation. He wanted to understand. He then returned to bed, leaving Grace alone again.

She finished her drink and returned to bed as well, and fell quickly asleep with the gentle rocking of the waves.

She sent Kevin all the links to the videos of Bart Millard and MercyMe speaking of the story behind his songs as Jeff had done for her. Over the next few weeks, they went out for an afternoon jaunt on the sailboat several times. He shared with her about his Catholic upbringing, but for over 20 years had removed himself from the Church. They discussed the videos and music of *Welcome to the New*. They discussed verses of promise and what they meant. They shared their life's aspirations, and over time their dreams took shape. They talked of Yehovah. And Grace learned to sail.

11 | Just a Turtle

Early March

The winter months passed quickly with spring well underway in Victoria. Kevin took the last few months to get all the sailing certificates he required to teach and certify people in several levels of sailing. He formed a corporation, built a business and marketing plan, and tapped into his network to promote his new business.

His calendar was booked fully into the late summer with charters, along with the work of starting his new enterprise. She saw little of him for about a month.

For Grace, the renovations completed on time and budget. The decorator finished her work. The kitchen supplies and food staples started to arrive. She placed an ad to hire kitchen and till staf,f and organized interview times. Connie arrived home a few days later to run the interviews. About one week of work remained in her contract with Connie.

Although she had contacted business friends about soon being available, looked for work, and responded to posted jobs, nothing came in.

She saw her circumstances becoming much like last fall when she lost her job with no open doors visible. But her Yehovah already provided regardless of the lack of evidence. This dark thing arose in her path, but she now saw only a turtle, not a shark.

She rested in her trust that Yehovah looked after her. She prayed about her needs and unlike last time, she filled with peace despite life throwing a storm her way. Last time, this tempest, this hurricane, ripped her thoughts and emotions to shreds.

Not this time. No storm or crisis arose that Yehovah was not aware of. He already cleared a path. She let the wave wash under her surfboard and laughed. Nothing to see here but a passing turtle.

Now, when she dug into the promises, she knew Yehovah saw her as His flawless, cherished and dear child. She knew He always fulfilled His promises. When she entrusted her life to Him, she knew He would always act in her favour.

For a moment, fear would enter her mind, but she prayed in the name of Yeshua for a greater measure of faith, trust, and courage to stand firm against any fear the storms of this life could bring.

Several weeks passed with no open doors, no work opportunities, but Yehovah filled Grace's mind with faith beyond understanding and her heart with an abundant joy. She couldn't explain it all, but decided best to not dwell on it. She risked concluding this gift of peace and her behaviour resided in the realm of irrational, and if irrational, she'd be required to pick up the burden of worry.

In the meantime, she successfully sold her images online and used this between-jobs time to wander the city and beachfronts, adding to her photo collection.

Mid-April

Grace arrived home after a good afternoon with Abbey and her camera, and picked up her messages to find Kevin called.

He invited her out for dinner that evening, leaving her a short time to get ready. They went to the Aura Waterfront Restaurant and sat at one of the best patio tables overlooking the harbour. The warm evening eased into night. The sunset painted the sky in rich reds and oranges.

They enjoyed a leisurely meal with easy conversation. They chatted about his business and all the different groups of people who signed up for weekend and weeklong sails.

Over coffee he leaned forward, looked her in the eye and said, "Listen, Grace, I don't know if this is something you would be interested in, but I would like to contract you part-time. I am way too busy and really need help with the organization and administration stuff. I have watched how you handled the contractors and work for Connie, and think you would be a perfect fit. I think I only need someone part-time and I don't know if this would work for you. But I would pay you well." Putting on his most charming smile, he said, "And I would like to keep you close. You make me think, and all this thinking has been a good thing. So, what do you say?"

They talked of the details of the work, the amount of time and the pay. He offered a generous deal and she, rather excited at the opportunity, agreed to start the following week. They both leaned back in their chairs, contented to watch the sky artistically progress to night.

Looking out over the lights reflecting in the harbour, she thought about the ocean – this space between land and sky. What a magnificent representation of the living water (Yeshua) who bridges the gap between the land of humanity and the sky of Yehovah. Interesting – the only day of creation the Lord refrained from declaring good occurred when the heavenly firmament separated from the earth below. Yehovah could never declare separation as good. Then the living water came and bridged that gap.

She loved the water and would eternally. She jumped into this living water, leaving behind the rationality of humanity and floated in His care, unburdened by the storms of life.

Ah, yes. She was living the flawless life.

The End

Thank You

I hope you found *The Flawless Life* an inspiring story. Many people have shared with me how the story touched their life. I would encourage you to leave a review to help other readers decide on this book! Your review is gold to an author and I love hearing your thoughts.

If you'd like to be notified of new book releases sign up at SerenityMcLean.com/author-updates/

I'm always looking for people interested in reading an advance copy of a book in exchange for an honest review. If that is you, please sign up at SerenityMcLean.com/author-updates/ and I'll be in touch.

You can also visit SerenityMcLean.com for her full list of great fiction.

The Flawless Life

Heartwarming and Inspiring Collection

Weeping Dune
Chapter 1

She hid in the dark bathroom, sobbing. Waiting. Listening. Quiet finally ruled the hotel room for at least an hour. She came to a decision. Cowering in the darkness gave her plenty of time to think. She finally had enough. The rocky relationship had crossed her line. Anders scared her. Now she needed to wait until he fell into a drunken sleep to quietly slip away.

Some vacation, she thought bitterly. *How could it go so badly on the first day?* She thought they both committed to use this vacation to get their relationship back on track. She pledged to let go of the pain and give her whole heart to a new start. Instead she found herself with fresh emotional wounds, and if Anders hadn't been drunk, he probably would've landed that first blow.

She had struggled a long time with his psychological attacks, thinking she was weak and too sensitive. She thought she needed to toughen up. And she would've continued trying to shrug off his targeted torment, except assault crossed her line. She would not be anyone's punching bag.

Sitting in the dark on the cold bathroom floor, she thought it a perfect echo of her broken heart. A room with a toilet was the perfect place for her to call an end to the relationship. Finally, she stood up, stiffly, strength and fear pounding in her head.

She listened at the door, holding her breath to hear every sound. She was sure she heard heavy, steady breathing. She listened for another minute. She needed him to be in a deep enough sleep to grab her purse and at least her carry-on.

There was a deep snore, then back to heavy breathing. Quietly, slowly, she opened the door and peeked through the crack. The room was slightly lighter than the bathroom. He must have left the curtains open. *That should provide enough light to find my stuff and get out.*

With a pounding heart she decided it was now or never. She did not want to face him in the morning. It would be filled with a twisting of the truth and another compromise on her part. *Never again.*

With the door partly open, she paused briefly, ready to close it quickly if needed. All she heard was his deep, rhythmical breathing. She stepped through the vanity area and waited another five heartbeats before looking around the corner to the bed.

Read about how God can restore what
life's locusts have eaten!
Now available both in paperback and ebook.

Leaving Lost
Chapter 1

She had just enough time to stop and say a final goodbye before catching her flight back home. She stepped out of the car and opened her umbrella. The drizzly, grey day reflected her heart. Looking toward the back of the old church lot, she let out a deep sigh. For two years she'd refused to let go. She navigated through the cemetery to a quiet spot overlooking the River Don. She laid flowers on the grave and sat down cross-legged on the wet grass. It felt like it had been raining for years.

"I'm sorry, Andrew, but I have to leave. I'm probably not ever coming back so –" She choked on her rising sobs. She pulled out a tissue and held it over her eyes. Her heavy heart let out its pain.

Looking up the river she thought, *I'm going to miss this place, but I've held on too long to the past.* She ran her hand over the blades of grass remembering their days together – sweet days of hope and dreams.

Well, those sunny days of love are long gone forever. Death ripped my happily ever after from me.

She looked back at the gravestone, pulling her mind from what could have been back to the present. "Mom needs me now and I have to go. I guess this is goodbye. I love you, Andrew. I always will." She stood up, leaned forward and kissed the stone marker. She turned and walked away from her soul mate.

Read about God's faithfulness
even in the darkest of days
in Leaving Lost.
Now available in paperback and ebook.

The Flawless Life

Final Moments Series

Have you thought about how crazy things are getting? The young horses of the apocalypse are stomping and snorting. They are galloping on the edges of the world getting ready for their riders to storm across the pages of history.

Rainswept

Mystery. Medical intrigue. Awakening of a lost relationship.

A trail of unexplained deaths and impending environmental collapse lead a beautiful doctor to the shores of the Baja, a suspicious surfer, and a long overdue confrontation with her sister.

Read about when God leads straight into fiery places –
those places we prefer to avoid –
to bring us to healing and restoration

Veiled Agenda

Marina's life takes an exciting turn as she escapes a political coup and faces increasing danger on the trail of Malthusias. Will he succeed in his promise to put an end to her? Or will she finally expose his veiled agenda?

Marina is the target of the one man
determined to eliminate
a quarter of the world's population.
The sickly green horse is warming up.

The Flawless Life

Don't Forget

Bonus Content

Don't forget to check out the bonus content on my website. There is a short story of a life-changing event for both Kevin and Grace and book discussion at www.serenitymclean.com/flawlessbonus/. Use the password welcometurtles to access.

The Flawless Life

About the Author

Serenity, born in Ontario, now lives in Western Canada. She spends many, many hours thinking about God, prophesy, eternity and what it will be like. Her life and relationship with God inspires the stories in the Heartwarming and Inspiring Collection. And her thoughts of prophesy spark the stories in the Final Moments series.

As a "pantser" author (writing by the seat of her pants), she doesn't start with an outline, but simply writes the story. When starting, she knows the beginning and how things will look at the end, but everything in the middle reveals itself as she writes. She meets each new character only when they enter the story and wonders what role they will play.

"I don't know if there are many authors like me, but I close my eyes and the story plays out like a video in my head. Then I write down what I've seen."

You can find out more about Serenity on her website at www.serenitymclean.com.

The website shares Serenity's inspiration (music, images, and links) for each of her books, some free short stories, blog posts, a few book reviews, and a scrapbook of web content she likes.

Serenity also connects with readers on FaceBook, even running contests to win a free copy of a book.

Don't forget to sign up to be notified of new releases or become a book reviewer and access bonus content.

Get in touch as she loves to talk about her books, current events and the prophetic timeline. She looks forward to hearing from you.

Connect with Serenity:

Blog: www.serenitymclean.com/blog/

Twitter: https://twitter.com/SerenityMcLean_ (note the underscore at the end)

Pinterest: https://www.pinterest.com/mclean3963/

Facebook: www.facebook.com/Serenityauthor

YouTube: https://www.youtube.com/channel/UCt82lzlc7NDixFAH-fuFZXfg

JD Farag

JD is actually a real person living in Kaneohe, Hawaii and is my online pastor. You can find him at www.youtube.com/user/alohabibleprophecy. He is a wonderfully honest and humble guy teaching on the entire Bible. He delivers an important message of hope in these days of global unrest and uncertainty. Each week he uploads videos from his Thursday Bible study, the Sunday service and the Prophesy Update to his YouTube channel. All are great and well worth watching.

If you are wondering *if* you are going to heaven, JD has a good news message for you.

The Good News of Salvation in Jesus Christ

The good news of salvation in Jesus Christ is also known as the Gospel, which means good news, your debt has been paid in full and you've been set free. However, in order for the good news to be good, there must also be bad news to make that good news good. Thus we need the bad news first. So what's the bad news? Thankfully, the Bible is not silent concerning both the bad news and the good news.

The Bad News

Romans 3:10. As it is written: "There is no one righteous, not even one…

Romans 3:23. …for all have sinned and fall short of the glory of God…

Romans 5:12. Therefore, just as sin entered the world through one man, and death through sin, and in this way death came to all people, because all sinned…

Romans 6:23a. For the wages of sin is death…

John 3:3. Jesus replied, "Very truly I tell you, no one can see the kingdom of God unless they are born again."

The Good News

Romans 6:23b. …but the gift of God is eternal life in Christ Jesus our Lord.

Romans 5:8. But God demonstrates his own love for us in this: While we were still sinners, Christ died for us.

Romans 10:9–10. If you confess with your mouth, "Jesus is Lord," and believe in your heart that God raised him from the dead, you will be saved. For it is with your heart that you believe and are justified, and it is with your mouth that you profess your faith and are saved.

Romans 10:13. "Everyone who calls on the name of the Lord will be saved."

When you fully understand the bad news, you'll want to hear the good news and call on the name of the Lord, confessing with your mouth that "Jesus is Lord," and believing in your heart that God raised Him from the dead. Then, if and when you do this, the Bible promises you will be saved and have everlasting life.

John 3:16. For God so loved the world that he gave his one and only Son, that whoever believes in him shall not perish, but have eternal life.

Here is an example of how you can call on the Lord and accept Jesus Christ's payment for your sin, which He paid for in full with His death on the cross and His resurrection from the dead:

"Dear Lord Jesus, I know I am a sinner. I believe in my heart that You died for my sins, and I confess with my mouth that you rose again from death. I accept you as my Lord and Savior. Thank you for saving me. Amen."

Again, this is only an example of how you can call on the Lord and be saved. This is the most important decision you will ever make. When you make this decision, the Holy Spirit will indwell you and empower you to live a holy life. Then, when He does, you will find you no longer desire the things of your old life. Instead, you'll have a desire to read the Bible, which is the Word of God, and you'll also desire to go to church and fellowship with the people of God, this because you are now born again of the Spirit of God.

JD Farag

Thanks, JD!

If you have accepted Jesus Christ's payment for your sins and now live with Him as your Lord and saviour, both JD and I will see you in heaven! Remember no eye has seen, no ear has heard, nor has it entered into the imagination of any human the great things in store for those who belong to Him. Think big because it will be better than that!

The Flawless Life

The Flawless Life

www.ingramcontent.com/pod-product-compliance
Lightning Source LLC
Chambersburg PA
CBHW051308170626
46809CB00004B/1797